Jubilation Grove
and
Other Nightmares

By Sarah Matthews

Copyright 2022 Sarah Matthews
All rights reserved.
Paperback ISBN: 979-8-9857200-0-6
eBook ISBN: 979-8-9857200-1-3
Edited by Kate Nascimento
Author photograph by Wade Carter Photography
Cover Art by Grim Poppy Design
Formatted by Michelle River

Stories

ALTERNATE REALTY

"This is the foyer," the realtor said, ushering Dave into the house.

Cheery yellow wallpaper adorned the walls, reflecting slightly off the light hardwood floors. Then he noticed a black stain in the top corner of the room. "What's that?"

"Oh, it's nothing you can't paint over," said the realtor, waving a dismissive hand. "Or it's a spider web. Or creeping rot. Nothing to worry about. Come on, there's so much more to see!" She grabbed Dave's arm and pulled him further inside.

The realtor led Dave through the house, showing him room after room in quick succession. In just a few minutes, Dave saw a living room with a vaulted ceiling as high and ornate as a cathedral, a sunken dining room, a kitchen with lime-green counters and brown cabinets, and a bathroom with a cracked concrete floor and brown shag carpeting on the ceiling; all papered in the same bright-yellow wallpaper as the foyer, and all with the same disconcerting black stain lurking somewhere inside them.

After these relatively common spaces, the realtor took Dave through the less typical rooms.

"This is the orangery," she said, as they entered a glassed-in room full of orange trees, drooping with overripe fruit. The stench of rotting citrus made Dave gag.

"I don't think this is the right house for me," he gasped, covering his nose and mouth with his free hand.

"Don't make up your mind until you've seen the whole house!" said the realtor, her smile wide and predatory. "Come on."

The next room was full of steel shelves lined with glass jars. "We're in the homunculatory now," she said. The jars were filled with tiny humanoid figures floating in colored liquid.

"This is the bibliopanopoly," said the realtor in the next room. Bookcases overflowing with moldering tomes dominated the room, arrayed in a maze-like pattern. The floor revolved like a carousel. Dave staggered and fell into one of the bookcases, sending an avalanche of books tumbling down on him.

"Here's the Doll Room," panted the realtor as she rushed through a door into another yellow wallpapered room, empty save for a single naked doll—a baby with only short tufts of hair remaining—sitting in the corner facing the wall. Before the realtor slammed the door shut behind them, the doll's head rotated to face him. Its face was covered in black rot.

The realtor kept a death grip on Dave's hand as they ran

down a seemingly endless hallway. The wallpaper blurred into a jaundiced smear. Their feet pounded with muffled thuds on the arterial red carpet, which was patterned with black, screaming faces. Dave recognized one of them was his.

Finally, they reached a boarded-up door at the end of the hallway. From behind it emanated a shrill, high-pitched sound—a combination of a power saw, a fax modem, and a bloodcurdling human scream.

"Sorry, that doesn't come with the house." The realtor reached up and pulled a cord hanging from the ceiling. A set of stairs slid down from above with a crash, nearly bashing Dave in the head. The realtor shepherded him up the steps.

"The attic!" she yelled as they emerged into the only room so far that wasn't wallpapered. Instead, plaster had been haphazardly scraped across the walls, and all the corners had been filled in so no ninety-degree angles remained. Random phrases, paragraphs, and diagrams crept across the rough surfaces. "BEWARE THE HOUNDS!" repeated itself most often.

Dave spun in a circle, trying to take everything in. He wound up face-to-face with the realtor. Her eyes now bulged wildly, hair floating around her face like a mane.

"This could also be a great bonus space for the kids..." she growled. She wrapped her arms around him and flung herself backward through the attic opening, pulling him with her. Dave screamed and braced himself for a fall, but he and the realtor were somehow standing upright again.

His head swam as he tried to comprehend the shift in perspective. They stood in a basement the size of a ballroom. The wallpaper had resumed its tyranny down here, but thick black tendrils of ooze snaked down the walls, making them look like they were melting.

The realtor hunched over and galloped off on all fours. Dave ran after her, not eager to be abandoned in this hellhole.

"FULLY FUCKING FINISHED BASEMENT!" screamed the realtor in a high, insectoid trill that reverberated off the walls. She skittered across the room. Upon reaching the opposite wall, she clambered up it and perched in the corner.

Dave stared in horror as her mouth widened and elongated until her jaws reached from floor to ceiling. Her teeth lengthened into fangs and black drool fell from her lips onto the floor.

"EXTRA STORAGE IN THE CRAWL SPACE!" she roared, black spittle flying from her mouth as her massive teeth gnashed together.

She lunged at him. He screamed and jumped sideways to avoid her maw, banging painfully against a small door in the wall. It had to be the crawl space. A way out maybe. He yanked the door open and scrambled inside, pulling the door shut behind him. It buckled and rattled in its frame.

He turned around and crawled away. The spongy floor sagged beneath him. Moisture dripped down the heaving walls.

Suddenly, the floor gave way and he fell into a tarry

pit of the black ooze which permeated the house. The pit walls pulsed and constricted around him. He struggled to keep from drowning in the mire, but it just kept pulling him down.

"I see you found the indoor pool," the realtor's voice whispered from everywhere and nowhere. "I hope you enjoyed your tour. Please see yourself out. If you'll excuse me, I have another potential buyer to greet."

Dave tried to scream, but the ooze poured into his mouth, suffocating him. The last thing he heard was the realtor's far-off voice: "This is the foyer."

The Jeweled Mask

In the time of the plague, she wore a jeweled mask. Only her emerald eyes remained uncovered. Others wore masks as well, but none so elaborate or concealing as hers.

Once, a man approached her. He wore no mask because, she thought, he equated recklessness with fearlessness.

"Remove your mask," said he. "For such beautiful eyes must sit in an equally beautiful face. Do not fear the plague."

"This mask is for your protection, not mine.".

The man scoffed and removed it, He looked upon her visage, and fell down dead.

The woman sighed and pulled her mask back on.

Shamble On

I stood outside The Beckoning Darkness coffee shop, reading their menu board.

"Today is Shamble Appreciation Day," it read. "Show us your best shamble and get 20% off your order, plus a complimentary sense of unease that you've taken part in something you really, *really* shouldn't have."

I shrugged and hunched over, letting my arms dangle disjointedly. I shambled through the door.

Outside, the sky turned ashen, a wolf howled, and thirteen crows circled above the building. I shivered but continued shambling. The Beckoning Darkness made the best coffee in town, and their promotions were always worth the dire consequences.

Sunflower Lake

Kayla and Brooke trudged down the overgrown path through the forest, sweating in the blazing afternoon sun.

"Can we turn around now please?" said Brooke. "I'm about to get eaten up by these mosquitos and chiggers. Plus, I'm sweating so much my shorts are about to slide off my ass."

"I feel that," said Kayla, pulling up her own shorts. "We should have brought some bug spray. This is what we get for thinking we can just pull over on the side of some back country road and start hiking because we feel like it."

Brooke laughed. "I'm surprised we haven't been murdered by hillbillies by now. What were we thinking?"

"Let's sit down to rest for a bit and then we can head back to the car," said Kayla, sitting down on a large stump. Brooke joined her.

While Brooke fixed her hair, which had fallen out of her ponytail, Kayla stared vacantly off into the distance, trying to get her breathing back under control. As her heart rate returned to normal, a blaze of yellow through the trees caught her eye.

"What's that?" she said, pointing at the yellow blob in the distance.

"What, that yellow stuff?" asked Brooke. "I don't know. Don't really care. I just want to get back to the car."

Kayla stood up. "It's only a little ways off. C'mon. The most interesting thing we've seen on this hike so far was that squirrel with the skinny-ass tail."

Brooke arched an eyebrow at her.

"Oh, come on!" Kayla wheedled. "Look, if it's more than five minutes from here, we'll turn around and go back."

Brooke heaved a sigh and got to her feet. "All right, we can check it out."

They headed off further down the path, and in a few minutes, they had reached their destination. The bright yellow that had caught Kayla's attention turned out to be a ring of sunflowers almost six feet tall, surrounding a huge, brilliant-blue pond. The only gap in the circle of sunflowers was where a pebbly beach led down to the water. On the beach was a white rowboat.

The women pulled out their phones and began taking pictures. After a few minutes, Kayla said: "You wanna get in the boat? I could take us around the lake."

"Do you even know how to row a boat?" asked Brooke.

"How hard can it be?" said Kayla, pushing the boat out into the water. She clambered in and sat on the bench with the oars. Then she patted the other seat, beckoning for Brooke to join her.

Brooke rolled her eyes. "Fine, but when your arms fall

off from rowing, don't come crying to me." She climbed in and sat opposite her friend.

"Hey, if my arms fall off, you're going to have to row us back," Kayla replied.

"No way," Brooke said, laughing. "I'm going to make you row back with your feet. I ain't doing a damn thing. This was your idea!"

"Whatever," said Kayla. She grabbed the oars, and after a few false starts, managed to get the boat moving. They wavered their way across the pond, sometimes going in a circle, sometimes zigzagging drunkenly due to Kayla's lack of rowing skills, both of them laughing so hard they almost fell out of the boat several times.

By the time they had reached the middle of the pond, Kayla had to stop. "Man, I've going to have the buffest arms when I'm done with this. Everyone's going to be super jealous of me and you're going to wish you'd rowed some."

"Who am I to rob you of buff arms?" Brooke replied. "I'm not rowing back, no matter what you say."

"Be that way then. But let me rest for a minute before we head back."

"Sure."

They just sat in the boat for a while, silently admiring the scenery. The ring of sunflowers blocked the view of the forest they'd been walking though, except for where the pebbled beach broke up the wall of yellow. Puffy clouds rolled by, reflected in the pond. A gentle breeze rippled the water. From the opposite bank, a trio of deer emerged: two adults and a fawn.

Brooke saw the deer first and excitedly pointed at them. "Oh my God, look! It's deer!"

Kayla whipped around to look. "Aah! They're so cute! I just want to row over there and steal them!"

"I don't think we can fit three deer into a boat with us," said Brooke.

Kayla laughed. "Always killing my dreams."

Then, to their surprise, the deer stepped into the water and began wading out toward them. As the water got deeper, the deer began to swim toward the middle of the lake.

"I didn't know deer could swim," said Kayla.

"Well obviously they can, because they're doing it," said Brooke. "I just can't believe they're getting this close to us."

As the deer drew closer to the boat, Kayla and Brooke held their hands out. The deer didn't shy away, but nor did they approach. Instead they continued paddling straight ahead. The women trailed their fingers over their soft fur as they passed and watched as they glided gracefully away, heading for the opposite shore.

As they watched, the buck disappeared under the water, pulled down so quickly it didn't even have time to make a sound. The doe and the fawn each let out a startled bleat and began swimming back the way they had come. Then the doe was pulled under the surface, just as swiftly as her mate. The fawn panicked and tried to swim back to shore even faster, but it too was yanked into the depths.

Kayla and Brooke both screamed.

"Oh my God, what happened to them?" yelled Kayla.

"I don't know! Row us closer," said Brooke. "Maybe we can help them."

Kayla grabbed the oars and rowed frantically to the spot where the deer had sunk. There was nothing to suggest any kind of struggle below the surface; no churning water, not even any air bubbles.

"Where'd they go?" asked Kayla.

Brooke scanned the water for any sign of the animals.

"Do you see them?"

"No. Why don't you help me look?" snapped Brooke.

They both leaned over the side of the boat and peered into the depths of the pond. Unlike the rest of the water, which had been relatively shallow, this area had to be quite deep. The water was so dark it was almost black. They stared into it, unable to look away.

"How deep do you think it is here?" said Kayla.

"Pretty deep," Brooke replied.

"Do you think we could swim down deep enough to reach the deer?" said Kayla, leaning further over the side of the boat.

"No!" Brooke sat up at looked at Kayla now. "Something grabbed those deer, and I don't want to find out what it was. Get us back to shore!"

"Just a moment. Here, look at this." Kayla pointed into the water.

Bubbles had begun rising to the surface of the lake. The women leaned closer to investigate their source. Focused on the depths, neither woman noticed the boat beginning to shift.

The bubbles increased. Something was rising swiftly to the surface. Kayla and Brooke strained to see what it was. The boat then reached its tipping point and spilled the women into the frothing water.

As they struggled and tried to hold onto the boat, headless, bloody deer carcasses popped to the surface like corks around them. The women screamed. Kayla's flailing hand connected with the fawn's glistening corpse and she panicked, splashing away from the horrific site. Brooke was hyperventilating, frozen with terror. Kayla grabbed her arm and pulled her back to the boat.

Kayla boosted Brooke into the boat and was about to climb in herself when she noticed the oars floating a few feet away. She paddled over and grabbed one, then tossed it into the boat. As she reached out for the other oar, a gaping maw ringed with scores of hooked teeth rose out of the water to envelop her right arm. It pulled her beneath the water before she could scream.

"Kayla!" Brooke yelled. She jumped into the water after her and grabbed the other oar, ready to use it as a weapon if need be. Before she dived underwater, Kayla splashed back to the surface. Her face was pale and haunted, and her right arm had been gnawed off up to her elbow. The blood was billowing out into a huge cloud in the water, and a white knob of bone protruded from the wound.

Brooke grabbed her under the armpits and managed to pull her back to the boat. It took every ounce of energy Brooke had to boost her back in, because Kayla was quickly going numb with shock. When Kayla was in, Brooke managed to heave herself over the side, rolling onto the bottom of the boat with a painful thud.

"Kayla, stay with me!" she yelled.

Kayla's eyes fluttered open. "I guess you're gonna have to row back after all," she muttered, with a weak laugh.

"That's fine," said Brooke, taking off her belt. "That's fine. I got you. Just stay with me."

She wrapped the belt around Kayla's arm and yanked it tight. Kayla winced and cried out in pain.

"Sorry! I'm sorry! But I have to do it."

After making sure Kayla was secure, Brooke grabbed the oars and began rowing back to shore. The water churned, and waves splashed into the boat. From the depths arose a pair of black, lidless eyes on thick stalks. Brooke screamed.

The eyes were blocking the quickest route back to the shore. She tried to steer around them, but whatever creature the eyes belonged to kept maneuvering to block her path. And worse, the eyes moved closer to the boat.

Eventually, they hovered slightly above the women's heads. Brooke uttered a primal yell and rammed one of the oars into the right eye of the creature. Black goo oozed from the wound as she pulled the oar back and prepared to strike at the other eye. But a high-pitched shriek emanated from beneath the water and the eyes slid back under the waves.

Brooke rowed as fast as she could to get the boat back to the beach. She clambered ashore and helped Kayla drag herself out of the boat. She had just helped Kayla to her feet when waves began breaking violently against the shore. Another high-pitched shriek echoed through the air. The women turned around.

The creature fully emerged from the lake. It most closely resembled a giant crab—with a chitinous shell, two large pinchers, and eight smaller legs—but was also around six feet tall and had a mouth ringed with hooked teeth going down into its throat.

Skittering forward, it swiped a pincher at the women. They ducked out of the way.

Brooke set Kayla down on the beach and grabbed the oar again.

"Not today, fucker!" she yelled.

She jabbed the oar at its uninjured eye, but it bobbed out of her reach. Desperate, Brooke began whacking the creature wherever she could, trying to find a chink in its armor. But the oar kept rebounding off its shell, and eventually, with a click of its pincher, the creature snapped it in two. Brooke stumbled backward, tripped over a rock, and fell. The creature dove down toward her.

From the creature's blind side, Kayla jumped in front of it, wielding the other oar. She jammed it deep into the creature's left eye, leaving it a ruined mess. The creature shrieked and began clawing trying to remove the oar.

"Fuck you!" yelled Kayla, picking up a large rock with her remaining arm. She flung it wildly, hitting the creature in the mouth and knocking out several of its teeth.

"Yeah, fuck you, you bastard!" yelled Brooke. She

pulled herself up and began hurling rocks with her friend. Finally, the creature began to scrabble backward into the lake, mewling and flailing its pinchers, then disappeared below the surface.

The women stared at the lake, where the only sign of the creature that remained—apart from the deer carcasses still floating in the water—were a few small waves lapping along the beach. Kayla and Brooke looked at each other, then burst out laughing in relief.

"We kicked that thing's ass!" said Kayla.

"Hell yeah, we did!" Brooke agreed. "High five!"

Kayla glared at her. "Really?"

"Sorry! I forgot!"

The two of them turned and began walking back to the trail, Brooke helping Kayla as needed.

"You forgot that a fucking crab monster ate my arm?" said Kayla.

"Look, I said I was sorry!"

As the women made it back to the trail, the water exploded behind them. With dread filling their hearts, they turned back to see a twelve-foot crab monster emerge from the lake. Its eyes darted around for a moment, then fixed on the women.

It roared. The women ran.

Self-Reflection

"Your greatest fear lies within this room." So said the sign on the ornate red door.

Shrugging, I opened it and stepped inside. My reflection stared back at me from a golden mirror. The door slammed shut behind me.

"Really? A mirror? I get it. My greatest fear is myself," I drawled sarcastically.

My reflection smirked. "Yes. You *are* your greatest fear. Because you know what you've done. You know what you're capable of. And you know what you *will* do..."

It reached out of the mirror, and hands identical to mine wrapped around my throat.

Something's Here

Kate stood on the mansion's decrepit wooden stairs, her hands clamped over her eyes.

"Nothing's there," she whispered repeatedly. "Nothing's there."

But still she could feel a presence behind her, could hear the faint groan of wood under a barely perceptible footstep. The presence drew closer. Kate couldn't stand it. She spun around and uncovered her eyes.

Nothing there.

Behind her, a step cracked like a gunshot. She turned to see a shadowy figure arching itself over the banister from the inky blackness of the first floor below. It grinned sardonically at her, clambering disjointedly forward. She screamed.

FOOTSTEPS

When I was six years old, I found out my grandparents' old house on Briarwood Lane was haunted. I'd always suspected it, but at that age, I suspected everywhere was haunted at night. I'd always spend a week or two at the rambling old Victorian house in the summer. I had a room all to myself, full of toys. Outside there was a huge fenced-in yard with a swing attached to an oak tree, and a turtle sandbox for me to play in.

Back then I wore leg braces at night—clunky, white plastic contraptions with myriad straps and buckles I could never hope to undo by myself. They weighed at least fifteen pounds just by themselves, roughly a third of my own body weight. I hated those things so much. Every night I fought and cried not to wear them, but I always lost.

One night, I woke up suddenly. I couldn't tell what had awakened me. I lay in bed and scanned my room. Moonlight streamed in through the sheer curtains, illuminating the middle of the room, my bed, and the doorway, which was located on the wall opposite. Shadows draped the corners of the room, so naturally that's where I figured any ghost would lurk. I stared into the dark, searching for signs of anything unnatural, ready to dive under the covers for protection at any moment.

So intent was I on finding monsters in my bedroom that I barely noticed the sound until it happened again—a soft footstep on the stairs leading up from the first floor. My attention turned from the bedroom to the staircase. The noises were faint, making just enough sound to register as footsteps. My heart thudded in my chest as fear crept over me. These weren't my grandparents' footsteps. My grandparents were asleep in the bedroom down the hall. Also, I would have heard if they had gone downstairs for some reason. The stairs were old, and they creaked and groaned under my weight, let alone the weight of an adult. Who or what could produce such a light tread?

The footsteps continued their soft approach. Up the stairs they came, then paused for a moment. I hoped they'd stopped for good, but they soon resumed their treading. Down the hall they came, past my grandparents' room and toward my open door. I yanked the covers up over my head and squinched my eyes shut. In through the door they came, across my bedroom floor, their relentless low thumps stopping only when they were directly next to the head of the bed, where I lay cowering.

A rush of cold air swept over me and I shivered, despite my resolve to move as little as possible, to make as little noise as possible.

I couldn't tell you how long I lay there, in a silent stand-off with whatever had padded its insidious way into my room. The minutes stretched out until time became an endless Möbius strip of "now". My muscles shook faintly from the tension of trying to keep perfectly still. Drool slid out of the corner of my mouth and ran down my chin, pooling on my sheets. I didn't dare risk making a sound by swallowing. The weight of the unknown entity's stare felt oppressive, like a pillow pressed over my face.

After a torturously long time, the pressure lifted. I heard those soft, measured steps again, heading toward the door. They resumed their course back down the hallway. My breathing and my heart rate slowly returned to normal.

Then I made a mistake.

The air under the comforter was stifling, and I was overcome with claustrophobia, so I whipped the covers off from over my head and took a huge breath.

The footsteps stopped.

I didn't have time to move. I was too terrified to move. The footsteps began again, still soft, but no longer slow. Instead, they *raced* back down the hallway and into my room.

In an instant, a woman's face was thrust into mine, fast enough that the frigid breeze caused by her movement ruffled my hair. Her eyes were flat and white like a marble statue, and her crescent moon smile glimmered as she leered at me.

She reached out. Her hands radiated cold, and I knew if I let her touch me, I would die—either of fright or from her malicious intent. I screamed and rolled away from that grinning visage. My twin-sized bed didn't give me much room to maneuver, and the hated leg braces gave my fear-enhanced movement more momentum than usual. All this together led me to tumble off the other side of the bed.

I hit the floor with a crash, landing on my back. The air whooshed out of my lungs, leaving me gasping. Still, I managed to flip over onto my side. My fingers gripped the fibers of the shag carpet and I pulled myself across it as fast as I could until I was under the bed. The dust ruffle hung an inch or so from the floor, and I pulled it down as far as it would go. My fingers were on fire from carpet burn and my lungs were still aching, but my terror pushed these mundane pains aside. I couldn't hear the footsteps anymore, but I would have struggled to hear anything over the thudding of my heart and my involuntary whimpering.

Suddenly, the dust ruffle was pulled up out of my hands and a woman's face appeared before me. I let out a wheezing yell before I realized it was my grandmother. I burst into tears of relief.

"What's wrong?" she asked.

Even at six, I knew she wouldn't believe me if I told her I saw a ghost, so I invented a more plausible story. Through tears, I told her, "I had a really bad dream. I fell out of bed and I got scared so I hid under here."

"Well, come here, and I'll tuck you back in."

I scooted closer to my grandmother and she pulled me out from under the bed. With a bit of effort, on account of my bulky leg braces, she managed to scoop me up in her arms.

"Can I sleep with you and Grampa tonight?" I asked.

"You'll be all right once I get you back in bed. I'll tell you a story and you'll forget all about that bad dream."

I was beginning to believe my grandmother until I happened to look over her shoulder. The blood froze in my veins. The woman with the marble eyes smiled at me. I shivered. My grandmother must have assumed I was still shaken up over my bad dream. But then she turned around herself and came face-to-face the ghostly woman. Her grip on me tightened and she gasped.

My grandmother was a tough woman though. She took a deep breath.

"I think I'll let you sleep with Grampa and me just this once," she said, her voice barely shaking.

I closed my eyes as she carried me past the ghost. The other woman's glare fell upon me, and I could sense her frustration at my rescue. As my grandmother walked down the hall to her bedroom with me in her arms, faint footsteps followed behind us. I knew my grandmother could hear them too, because she quickened her pace and when she reached her bedroom, she rushed inside and shut the door so forcefully that it woke my grandfather.

Immediately, the ghost's influence lifted. My grandmother settled me down between her and my grandfather, who was still protesting being woken up at such an ungodly hour. I didn't think I'd be able to sleep, but I was so mentally and physically exhausted that I dropped off almost immediately.

I woke the next morning to the sun shining in through the bedroom windows, bathing me in a warm pool of golden light. Already, I was halfway to convincing myself that what happened really was a bad dream.

Sometime during the night, my grandmother had taken off my leg braces. I hopped out of bed, hoping that she would have a delicious breakfast waiting for me, but when I emerged into the hallway I found my grandmother out there, still in her pajamas. She was staring at their bedroom door, her expression unreadable.

"Whatcha lookin' at?" I asked.

"Do you see that?" she said quietly, pointing at the door.

I looked. Running down the door panel were long gouges, just barely visible. I gulped and nodded.

"OK. I suppose we'll have to repaint that before we move. Now what would you like for breakfast?"

That's the story of how I found out my grandparents' old house on Briarwood Lane was haunted, and also why it's their *old* house.

Hydra

Green blood spewed forth from the neck of the woman I'd beheaded. But the color of her bodily fluids was the least of my worries. I could think of three more pressing matters.

First: The woman was still alive.

Second: The blood that had spattered onto my steel-toed boots was now eating through them and burning my feet.

Third: Three more heads had sprouted, and all of them were laughing at me.

I grabbed my axe and swung wildly. Panting and covered in acid burns, I looked at what I'd achieved.

Hundreds of heads roared in unison. I ran.

The Librarian

Smoke hung thick in the air. Claire could just make out a Dewey Decimal number in it. The fire raged through the library, but Claire dodged through the flames until she reached the row of shelves she sought.

She ran down the aisle, tracking the numbers on the books. Eventually, she pulled a tome from the shelf: "IN CASE OF EMERGENCY".

Flames roared up the bookcase in front of her. She opened the book. A bright doorway appeared in the air. Claire stepped through it, closing the book as she did.

The door disappeared, and the library succumbed to fire.

Jubilation Grove

Trevor and Gwyn had been driving down verdant, tree-shrouded lanes for over an hour when Gwyn gently grasped Trevor's arm and murmured, "There. Pull in up there."

Trevor slowed down, squinting at the side of the road. "I don't see anything."

"Just pull over," said Gwyn, and with a sigh, Trevor pulled the car off onto the shoulder—though calling it a shoulder seemed a bit grand, considering it was only slightly mossier and more leaf-strewn than the road on which they had been traveling.

"Are you sure this is the place? It's just we've pulled over about half a dozen times and none of them have been right yet," he teased.

Gwyn smirked at him. "Of course this is the right place. I remember now. There's the boulder that looks like a funny little man crouching in the bushes, see?" she said, pointing off into the dense underbrush.

Trevor's gaze followed her finger. A large boulder squatted on the side of the road. It did look somewhat like a man, albeit one that was hunched in a disturbingly unnatural way.

Trevor was still puzzling about what precisely made the rock so disconcerting when he heard Gwyn click out of her seatbelt. She slipped out of the car and trotted around to the trees on the roadside before Trevor had time to unbuckle his own.

"Come on, dearie," Gwyn called, and Trevor found himself out of the car and following her before he knew what he was doing. "And don't worry about us getting lost," she said. "Once we're on the path, I could find the way blindfolded. I could find lots of places from this path if I wanted to. Some are easier than others to find. Jubilation Grove is the trickiest, but the best things in this world are often the most difficult. Luckily, you're with me, or you'd be hopelessly lost."

"Yes, lucky me," said Trevor, his gaze lingering on Gwyn's figure in her white cotton dress and thin sweater.

A deep throbbing swelled though his chest, but it wasn't due to Gwyn—at least he hoped it wasn't—for the sensation filled him with a deep feeling of foreboding. He felt his eyes drawn to the path that lurked ahead of them in the underbrush, although he couldn't see anything particularly out of the ordinary. And why did he think the path was lurking?

Gwyn's hand, pale and cool as alabaster, caressed Trevor's cheek and guided his face to hers. His unease grew as he looked into her slate-gray eyes, now large and solemn.

"This path starts the way to Jubilation Grove. Pay attention to me, because this is of dire importance," Gwyn said, her voice soft yet compelling. "As we venture down it, you must do as I say. If you won't do that, or think I'm joking, tell me now and we'll leave. I won't be upset if you tell me now, but if you disobey me once we're in there, you probably won't live to regret it."

A chill ran through Trevor's body, despite the warmth of the early spring afternoon.

"This path runs for about a mile though this forest," Gwyn continued, "and the trees are so dense overhead that we'll have to crouch almost the entire way. It's also known as 'the Deceitful Corridor,' because unless you're very careful, and say just the right cantrips in just the right way, it will take you all sorts of places you never intended to go. Since you don't know the cantrips, it is imperative that you don't speak. Do not ask questions, do not make comments, do not cry out, no matter what you may see or hear. Do not even think loudly. Silence the voice inside your mind. Focus on me, and on my voice. Follow my footsteps exactly, until I give you permission to do otherwise. Nod once if you understand and agree to these terms."

Trevor nodded.

"Good," said Gwyn. "Now follow me."

In one fluid movement, she bent down, parted the leaves of a low hanging branch, and ducked down onto the newly exposed path. She held the branch back for Trevor while he too shuffled under the trees.

Gwyn was right about the crouching. Trevor's neck began to cramp from keeping it bent so low as they continued forward. He was tempted to walk on his knees, or even crawl, but he felt it would displease her.

He tried to focus on Gwyn to take his mind off the physical discomfort and his growing sense of unease, but he found he couldn't bring himself to look directly at her. Instead, he carefully observed where she stepped, and tried to step in the same place.

Once, as they were rounding a corner, Trevor did hazard a glance at Gwyn. His heart leaped like a startled frog and he drew in a sharp breath to yell, but before he did, his eyes finally made sense of what he was seeing. Just a trick of the light. That was the only logical reason why Gwyn could have looked so unnaturally bent, even for someone crouching, why she seemed to move in such a strange manner. Trevor pushed those thoughts away as she began speaking.

"Thousands have trodden the path through these boughs, just as we tread it now. They trod it by day, and they trod it by night; in silken slippers, in fine leather boots, and in their bare, grass-stained feet. They all trod it, and they were all hunched over and creeping as we are now."

Trevor looked down at the path. Thick, mossy clumps lined the sides. The middle was a worn divot in the dirt, smooth and dark brown. Just wide enough for a person, or several people walking single file.

Despite the warmth of the day they'd left behind, the air in the Deceitful Corridor was cool. It smelled of leaves, of dampness, of aged things. The day had been bright and cloudless as they drove here. But based on the quality of light filtering in through the branches, the sky had since turned gray. Trevor heard no birds or insects or animals; no planes droning or cars racing by. It was as if all these sounds had been left behind on the road. The rustle of the leaves in the wind and their own movement through the branches were the only things he could hear now.

Suddenly, Gwyn began speaking in a strange, guttural language punctuated by hisses. Trevor's heart pounded as the underbrush around them began to thrash, as if at any moment, a horde of wild animals would burst through. The light through the trees turned the color of coal dust, and Gwyn's chanting rose in volume and intensity. Trevor panicked and turned to run, but as he did, a thick sense of lethargy fell over him like a pall.

The bushes had closed in behind them. And these bushes too, began to twitch and jerk, as if some large thing was making its own path directly to them.

With a frenzied shout from Gwyn, all movement in the underbrush ceased. The light returned to its green-tinged hue, and Trevor saw the path forming behind him again. He took several slow, deep breaths to steady himself. Then he turned to face Gwyn, a question forming on his lips.

Her pale face, partially veiled by a curtain of blonde hair, was less than an inch away from his. Gwyn's abrupt closeness made her face look uncanny at first, the face of some malicious forest sprite. Trevor bit his tongue to keep from screaming.

"You were thinking too loudly, weren't you?" Gwyn chided. She pressed a cool fingertip to his lips before he could answer. "I warned you about that. We're almost through the Deceitful Corridor, but 'almost through' is still partially in. Keep your mouth shut—your inner mouth especially, because it seems abnormally loud."

She withdrew her finger from his mouth, but Trevor still felt the lingering chill, as if it had been a stone against his lips rather than flesh. Gwyn pivoted back to the path and continued her crouched way through the forest.

Occasionally, she would do a little shuffling hop, as if leaping from stone to stone across a stream. Trevor followed suit as best he could, given the close quarters. Once, Gwyn threw herself flat on the ground. Trevor did likewise, and they wriggled along the path on their fronts for an interminable amount of time. Trevor's mind offered a feeble question about why he was doing this, but the question seemed distant and muted, and he noticed it only as one might notice the ticking of a clock in a far-off room. After the wriggling, there came more creeping, and after the creeping came movements he could not even have described. Gwen demonstrated these for him, and Trevor found himself mimicking her almost against his will.

Then Trevor squinted as he emerged from the dense underbrush into the relative brightness of a broad trail, where shafts of sunlight now pierced through the sparse canopy of leaves high above him. He hadn't realized how oppressive the air was in the Deceitful Corridor until he was out of it. This new path was like stepping into a pool, with a sense of near-weightlessness—not just physically, but spiritually as well.

As he floated along behind Gwyn, the sound of a rushing creek gradually grew louder ahead.

"You can speak now," said Gwyn. Hearing her talk at a normal volume after what had preceded made Trevor jump. When he looked at her, her lips parted in a smile that was more like a baring of teeth.

"Where are we?" asked Trevor. His voice came back to him sounding flat and lifeless, like the impersonal prerecorded message on a voicemail.

"We're headed for the Shamble," said Gwyn, her eyes flashing with excitement.

She grabbed Trevor's hand and pulled him along. Her excitement gave her a childlike air, and Trevor grinned, despite everything else that had happened. They dashed along this new path, the sound of the brook growing ever louder. The forest faded away for Trevor, his focus narrowing down to Gwyn's white-clad form, the way her body moved, and the way the sunlight shifted across her bouncing golden hair.

They proceeded this way for several minutes, which stretched and spun out like blown glass, morphing into something more than the sum of their parts. Eventually, they reached a low, crumbling stone wall. Gwyn sat down, then turned so that her legs were dangling over the other side of it. Trevor sat beside her, meaning to pivot around as well, but then he looked over the other side and his stomach went into freefall.

The wall overlooked the creek he'd heard for the last few minutes, but the water was at least a hundred feet below him. And worse, the cliffside beneath the wall was concave, so if he toppled over the side, there'd be no frantic scrabbling or clutching at rocks and roots to try and slow the fall. There would be just one long, helpless plummet. He stayed where he was, questioning his decision to follow a woman he barely knew down a strange woodland path.

Gwyn laughed as if she'd caught the flow of his thoughts. "Don't worry, I didn't bring you all the way out to the Shamble just to push you over the side. That'd be such a waste of a friend. Come over to this side with me."

Reluctantly, Trevor swung his legs over the wall to hang next to Gwyn's—hers scissored back and forth aimlessly, while his were poker straight.

"I need to give you instructions on how to get past this next section of the woods," she said, her gray eyes boring into him. "This is very important, so pay attention. Do you see those stairs over there?" She pointed off to her left, where a trail led to earthen steps shored up by rough-hewn stones. "Those stairs are called 'the Meditative'. And that isn't just a name, it's a commandment. As you traverse these stairs, you must meditate intently on one thing. Can you guess what that might be?" She arched an eyebrow at him.

"I don't know, your worst sin?" said Trevor. He'd meant the words as a joke, but as a zealous light flooded Gwyn's eyes, they turned into something real and writhed like serpents in his mouth.

"Yes, that's precisely right! If I didn't already know I'd made the right decision in bringing you here, that answer just confirmed it. Yes, you must think of the absolute worst thing you've ever done and meditate on that all the way down to the creek below. The creek is called 'the Slate Wallow', and spanning it is 'the Penitent's Pathway'. I should warn you, if we reach the Penitent's Pathway and you've not thoroughly meditated, or you've deluded yourself as to what your worst sin was, you'll never make it across." Gwyn folded her hands on Trevor's shoulder, placed her chin on her hands, and gazed coyly up at him. "So what's the worst thing you've ever done? Mind you, I'll know if you try to sell me on some half-hearted sin, and I'll be disappointed in you."

In that moment, it was if a cold hand closed around Trevor's heart, trapping it like a frightened bird. But he fought the urge to flee—not only because he had no place to run, but also because he still held onto the notion that wherever Gwyn was taking him would ultimately be well suited to sylvan sexual pursuits.

Thus, he quashed his reservations and told Gwyn of a girl he'd known in high school. She was unpopular, save for as a verbal punching bag for him and his friends. Trevor had been instrumental in crafting some of the worst nicknames and insults they'd used against her, and the girl had taken these epithets and internalized them, or so she'd said in a letter found after she'd slit her wrists. The girl survived but transferred to another school. Everyone knew that Trevor was part of the group that had tormented her, but the blame seemed to fall everywhere but on him. He faced no real repercussions for his actions, only an inchoate sense of guilt.

Gwyn, who had been listening avidly to Trevor's confession, clapped her hands in delight, the brisk sound echoing through the tree-shrouded overlook. "How utterly prosaic your sin is! It's so refreshing in its simplicity!"

Gwyn's dismissal of his darkest secret irked him. And so he said something he really shouldn't have. "All right, so what's your worst sin then?"

Gwyn's smile widened and her eyes gleamed with beatific joy as she told him.

Trevor knew that she had said words, and that they had been mostly in English, but he couldn't quite recall what she'd said. When he tried to think of it, his mind threw up error messages. 404 not found. He tried thinking past these mental blocks.

What had she said? It had involved... but now his brain was filled with a screech like a fax modem. Trevor stared off blankly into the distance for a moment that stretched out indefinitely.

Gwyn laughed impishly. "Oh dear, I've broken him! We can't have that now," she said, and kissed him full on the lips.

The kiss was warm and passionate. Her lips tasted of honey and their firmness against his own drove what she'd said even further out of his mind. Gwyn pulled away from the kiss first, then she grabbed Trevor's hand and pulled him up from the ledge.

"Come now. The daylight is wasting, and I want to get to Jubilation Grove before dark. It takes a very special person to tread these paths in the dark, and I'm not to that level yet."

"Is the rest of the path that dangerous at night?" asked Trevor.

"Oh dear, no. It's merely dangerous during the day. It's downright diabolical at night." She grinned again, and then pulled him toward the steps. "So come along then. And remember, you have to meditate on your worst sin or you'll never make it across the Penitent's Path."

Trevor tried to think about the girl he'd bullied in high school, but thinking about her disrupted his ideas about himself. He settled for thinking about how everyone was either a bit of an asshole or overly sensitive in high school. It was a phase you went through, no one's fault really. Some people got through it better than others, that's all. He was a decent guy now, so that made up for anything he might have done in his past.

Before he knew it, they'd reached the bottom of the stairs and stood on a path beside the swiftly running creek. The water was clear and deep. It was several degrees colder down here than up on the Shambles.

A series of thick slate stepping-stones spanned the creek ahead. They rose up out of the water, but still looked slick in places. Gwen stepped onto the first stone and held out her hand. Trevor took it and followed her as she hopped between them.

The panic didn't hit him until they'd almost made it across. A girl's sobs filled his mind and he jerked his head back and forth, trying to locate the source. Gwyn didn't seem to hear it. Trevor was rooted to the spot as a wave of self-loathing washed over him. The crying intensified, and Trevor let go of Gwyn's hand, using both of his own to cover his ears in a vain attempt to block out the sound.

Gwyn spun around. "Damn it! You didn't meditate properly, you ass! Don't move, I'll come get you."

Just then, the water surged up and covered the stones. It quickly rose to cover their ankles. Trevor noticed the rising water, but the rising despair in his mind overwhelmed him. Gwyn made her way back and reached out to put her arm around him when the water swelled again, nearly knocking her off the stone. She pinwheeled her arms, trying to regain her balance.

Trevor shook free from the despair that gripped him to grab hold of her before she fell. As she regained her footing, Trevor howled and let go of her again, grabbing his fore-arms. They burned like a razor had been raked across them. Overcome with pain, despair, and panic, Trevor sank to his knees.

The water raged higher still, threating to pull him off the stepping-stone and drag him downstream. Faintly, he could hear Gwyn yelling in the strange spitting language she'd used in the Deceitful Corridor. He wished the water *would* wash him away. It was a better ending than what he deserved. As he prepared to give in to it, the pain stopped abruptly, and the water receded.

"He is not yours to take!" Gwyn yelled.

The stepping-stones reemerged, and Gwyn pulled Trevor to his feet. She made him walk in front of her the rest of the way across the creek.

When they reached the opposite bank, Trevor turned to thank her for saving him, but quailed at the fury in her eyes. He had never seen such primal rage in a person before and he wondered if she was going to flat out kill him for his insolence. Gwyn must have sensed his fear, because her expression then softened to one of mere anger.

"That's what happens when you don't listen to me! Did you think I was playing games with you? That I was exaggerating when I said this path was dangerous?" she yelled.

"I'm sorry! All these rules and weird place names. It sounded like a joke. But what happened back there... That was real. And that was because I didn't meditate on my worst sin going down a set of steps?" Trevor shook his head. "I don't know what to say except I don't like this anymore. It's not cute, it's not funny. I don't know what it is, but I want to go back."

Gwyn arched an eyebrow at him. "Oh, you want to go back across the Penitent's Path? After what we just went through?"

"No, but there must be some other way back."

"The only way back is forward. Once we reach Jubilation Grove, there's a path that will take us out of the forest. Until then, you must follow my every instruction. Do you believe me now?" Gwyn asked.

Trevor nodded.

"Good. Now follow me."

They walked along an uphill path of packed dirt. Small roots stuck up from the earth like knobby fingers. Trevor made sure to mind where he stepped so he wouldn't trip.

"This part of the path is called 'the Cunning Mystery' because it leads to so many different places and no one knows quite how," Gwyn told him.

Trevor imagined there must be several paths that branched off the main one, which each led to different destinations. However, the path continued through the trees, the underbrush unbroken by any other trails. After a while, the path leveled out and came to what appeared to be a dead end at an enormous willow. Upon closer inspection, the path actually split in two, forming a circle around the willow and its weeping branches. On the opposite side from where they stood, the path seemed to continue much as it had before.

Gwyn pushed her way through the willow's dangling boughs to place her pale hand on the dark-brown tree bark and then caressed it. Trevor followed suit and put his hand on the tree. Instantly, he recoiled. The bark was clammy and too warm, like a fevered forehead. Gwyn took no notice of his discomfort and kept stroking the tree.

"This is the Impious Willow," she said fondly. "The heart of the Cunning Mystery. From here, we could access so many exciting places, if we had the time."

"I only see the one path," said Trevor. "How could we

access paths that aren't there?"

"Oh, they're there all right," said Gwyn. "Think of the Impious Willow as roundabout. We must go around the base of this tree in a precise fashion to reach our intended destination—take the exit for Jubilation Grove, if you will. So make sure you don't get off the path until I tell you, or there's no telling where you'll end up. Let's get going."

They stepped out from underneath the tree's shade and back onto the dirt path surrounding it. Gwyn led Trevor around the tree. Sometimes it only took a few seconds to walk the path around the trunk; other times it took several minutes. Trevor lost track of how many times they circled the tree, trusting that Gwyn knew where she was going. She certainly seemed to know what lay down each of the identical offshoot paths they passed.

"That way leads to Bramblemaw."

"Down there are the Lookers."

"Definitely don't want to get off here—it leads straight to Sleek Nellie's Grotto and then we'd be in real trouble."

Eventually, she remarked, "I can't say what lies down this path."

"You mean you've never been down there?" Trevor said, surprised.

"No, I've been down there many a time. I just can't *say* what lies down there." She lowered her voice to a whisper, full of awe. "It defies words."

Shortly after, she stopped so suddenly that Trevor almost ran into her. "Here we are."

The path in front of them had changed. Previously, it had looked like the path they were on—wooded, mossy, dusky. But now it was a grassy path that led between two massive rows of evergreen hedges. The hedges towered over them, at least twenty feet tall. They were perfectly groomed and yet so dense that Trevor couldn't see whatever was on the other side.

"This is the Looming Brood," said Gwyn, stepping onto the new path. "They guard the entryway to Jubilation Grove against any unworthy to enter. I had been afraid they might not part for you after what happened on the Penitent's Path, but as you can see, the way is clear. Follow me."

Trevor followed her onto the pathway, and they traveled in silence for a while. Eventually, Trevor said, "Who trims these hedges? It's weird to have such manicured hedges in the middle of the forest."

Gwyn turned back and smiled at him. "No one maintains the Looming Brood. No one could. They simply grow this way in deference to the path. But look! Jubilation Grove is upon us!" Her voice rose with a zealous fervor.

Trevor found himself in a forest of birch trees. But was "forest" the right word? It looked more like a park, since the trees were lined up in precise rows forming concentric circles, like headstones in a military cemetery, leading to a single vanishing point. Trevor's gaze followed down the pathway to Jubilation Grove's crowning feature.

At the center of the grove stood a moss-encrusted shrine containing a white marble statue. Trevor's rational mind saw and labeled these items clearly and logically, and it couldn't find anything to explain why terror fell over him like a shroud. From the moment Trevor laid eyes on the statue, he felt an anchor sink deep into his heart. The anchor dropped through every fiber of his being, eventually settling into his very core with a weighty thud as strong as his now-pounding pulse.

Oddly enough, he felt relieved. Here was everything he'd ever feared. Here was the embodiment of all the half-remembered nightmares, all the horrors that had ever haunted him, this thing that was both terrible and beautiful to behold. He realized that the statue had always waited here for him, that he had always unconsciously searched for it. All his life had led up to this moment. It felt like coming home.

Trevor knew without looking behind him that the Looming Brood had closed their ranks, forcing him onward to embrace his fate. He could feel the statue calling to him, the ominous foreboding of its presence like a deep, throbbing, monotone.

He turned to Gwyn, unsure if he should curse her or thank her. In the end, when she smiled and held out her hand, he simply took it and followed her.

As Gwyn pulled him down the aisle of birches leading to the statue, he felt like a fish being hauled to the surface of a lake, pulled irresistibly by a force it cannot begin to understand. Still the rational portion of his mind tried to assert itself, even as his irrational mind gibbered and his footsteps drew him inexorably toward the shrine. Surely he had nothing to fear from an old statue in the woods? Even, an *ancient* statue, in bizarre, otherworldly woods. No, Gwyn was the actual threat; her and whatever she had planned. She was obviously delusional. Maybe she planned to sacrifice him. If she had a knife, he could probably escape, maybe even get the knife away from her, force her to lead him out of the woods.

All these thoughts ran through his mind in the thirty or so seconds it took them to reach the shrine. Gwyn led him up the marble steps. The interior was cool and damp, and resembled a gazebo. Moss clung to the outside, but the inside was almost sterile in its cleanliness. As he approached the statue's base, a wave of primal fear subsumed any rational thoughts.

"Look upon Celaeno Mysichore, the Dark Huntress of the Dance," said Gwyn.

Trevor was powerless to do otherwise.

The marble statue took the form of a classically beautiful woman, shrouded from head to foot in folds skillfully carved to look like semi-sheer fabric. On her head was a crown of interwoven branches that twined together at the front to hold a carved bird skull. Arching above the crown, a pair of delicate antlers emerged from the woman's head. The woman's eyes were hidden from view by a veil, but her mouth could be seen. She was smiling, exposing a hint of pointed teeth. Trevor's stomach twisted in terror at the sight of that predatory smile.

The statue's left arm was extended in a graceful semicircle, like a dancer. From the outstretched arm, yards of draped fabric cascaded to the statue's base. The other hand clasped the trailing end of the figure's shroud and held it up, allowing one exquisitely formed leg to peek through. Trevor looked at that painfully beautiful limb and his heart welled up with despair.

"Isn't she stunning?" Gwyn said reverently.

Trevor jumped at her voice, which was right next to his ear.

"She is the culmination of all things. In centuries past, Jubilation Grove would be full of women leaping and wriggling in the Dance, and of the shouts of men as they dashed about during the Hunt. But eventually, the old ways died out. Soon there were fewer and fewer people to pay proper homage to the Dark Huntress. Now there's just myself in this, the land of her origin. But I do what I can. You should be honored. We will worship Her—I in The Dance, and you in The Hunt—and Jubilation Grove will once again be cloaked in praise!"

With this proclamation, Gwyn placed her hand on the hem of the statue's robes. An electric thrum coursed through Trevor's body. He watched in disbelief as a horrific change took place. Tendrils of tar-like, inky darkness emanated from Gwyn's touch and wound their way up the statue. They twined around the figure until it was jet black. The folds of its garments rippled, and ebony tentacles undulated to the floor of the shrine. A wave of nausea swept over Trevor as the statue's exposed leg stepped elegantly down from the plinth.

He stood transfixed in front of Celaeno Mysichore and might have stood there for all eternity had Gwyn not whispered, "Run, prey."

Trevor ran.

The birch trees blurred past him. He reached the Looming Brood. The path was still closed, but he tried to push through the hedges, heedless of the branches clawing his arms and legs. He was still trying to force his body through the dense shrubs when he sensed a presence behind him. He turned to see the outstretched fingers of Celaeno Mysichore less than a yard away from him.

Trevor staggered away from the hedges, a breathless, animalistic yelp escaping his lips. He ran around the perimeter of the grove, searching for any break in the thick hedges. Each time he stopped at a likely spot, he had only mere seconds before he felt Her cold breath on his neck or sensed Her grasping, reaching hands. Desperate, he turned and ran away from the hedges, zigzagging through the rows of birches on his way back toward the shrine.

At the base of the now-empty pedestal, Gwyn writhed frenetically in the throes of the Dance. Trevor ran toward her, arms outstretched. Gwyn, her eyes closed in bliss, paid him no mind. Trevor grabbed her by the shoulders and flung her backward down the steps. She let out a shriek as she fell. He shouted in triumph as he watched the undulating tendrils of darkness entangle her. But his relief was short lived. He watched in shock as they set Gwyn gently on the ground. Her grin was as sardonic as that of the dark entity next to her.

"Did you really think *you* could sacrifice *me*?" Gwyn said with a laugh. "Foolish boy, I am Her greatest acolyte. I bring Her tributes for the Hunt, and in return She rewards me beyond compare. Now, fulfill your role and be hunted."

The ebony-clad deity surged toward Trevor. He stumbled away, frantically looking for any sort of escape. His eyes fell on a previously unnoticed gap in the shrubs and he lunged toward it, arms and legs pistoning, ignoring the burning stitch in his side and the rasping pain in his lungs. He plunged into the opening, feeling Her icy aura tingling the hairs on the back of his neck. It led to a path bordered by the same dense shrubbery that surrounded the grove. Trevor ran on for a few more steps, then dared a glance behind him. He stopped running.

Celaeno Mysichore stood at the path's entrance, but her dark tendrils seemed to press up against an invisible barrier. Trevor laughed in relief, but he didn't like the way the entity continued to smile at him. He pivoted back around to follow the trail.

Dark-green light filtered through the bushes. Trevor followed the path, looking for offshoots or anything that felt familiar. But while the trail twisted and turned, it still consisted of the same impassible hedges. After several minutes, the path took a sharp left turn, leading him to… straight, even rows of birch trees. His heart sank like a stone dropped into a deep well.

Gliding toward him was the culmination of all his nightmares and terrors—the horrible and beautiful Celaeno Mysichore. Overcome with inevitability, Trevor fell to his knees, weeping and laughing. At the shrine, Gwyn leapt and contorted her body grotesquely, singing and hissing.

As She descended upon him, he raised his arms in praise, and Jubilation Grove lived up to its name once again.

Feeding Your Fears

It started small, with just a cookie here or there to appease the monster under the bed. But then the monster in the closet got jealous, as did the monster who clung to the ceiling, and soon the girl was feeding dozens of cookies to a trio of devoted demons.

The night the burglars came, the girl woke before her parents. She stood in the shadowy doorway, uncertain what to do. A burglar, sensing her presence, raised his gun.

Six glowing red eyes blazed in the darkness behind her. A clawed hand encircled her possessively. The burglars screamed.

DEAR DEMON IN MY HOUSE:

Thank you for whispering in my ear as I'm drifting off to sleep. It's quite soothing. I really enjoy your thought-provoking questions and comments, such as "What would your blood look like splattered on the wall?" and "Do you want to join the chorus of the damned?".

I also love how you rearrange my furniture. My couch is super heavy, and it flying across the room saves me the effort of moving it, plus it avoids scratching my hardwood floors. You have a real flair for design!

You are a valued addition to my home. Keep up the good work!

Predator and Prey

Estella whistled her way past the graveyard, an old superstition that nevertheless comforted her. Rumor had it that much more than spirits lurked in the cemetery nowadays. A foe, spoken of only in furtive whispers and always in the safest of places, had returned to plague their community.

Estella wasn't sure what to believe. True, several people had left town with no trace, but folks were more transient these days. Staying in one's hometown for longer than necessary, as Estella had, was gauche. But she knew this town intimately, knew all the secret routes and what lay down every street. Could any enemy of hers claim such knowledge?

Suddenly, a cry rang out from the graveyard. Estella froze, every muscle tense, every nerve alert. Perhaps the rumors had shaken her more than she believed. It was probably just a stray cat or something. She relaxed and resumed walking.

Then the cry came again, louder and longer this time. It wasn't a cat. It was a girl. What was a girl doing in the graveyard this late? Estella remembered her own youth spent sneaking out after curfew for reasons both innocent and not so innocent. Whatever had brought the girl here at this hour, she needed help.

The graveyard gate was locked, so Estella vaulted over the low brick wall surrounding it. She scanned through the tombstones, looking for the girl. There was another cry from somewhere on her left. She ran through the graveyard toward it, dodging monuments and headstones. After rounding a mausoleum, she found the girl.

She appeared to be about thirteen. She was swinging a stick at a man who looked to be in his forties. Estella recognized him. His name was Andrew, and he had a reputation for preying on the young.

Estella's face grew hot, and she had to take a moment to compose herself. She wanted to lunge at Andrew and dispose of him while she still had the chance to surprise him, but it was more important to get the girl to safety first. Then she could deal with Andrew.

Estella jumped out of the shadows and placed herself between the two of them, her arms outstretched. The girl screamed.

"Don't worry," said Estella, glancing over her shoulder at the frightened girl. "I'm here to help you."

"Stay out of this, Estella. This one's mine," Andrew growled. A snarl curled his upper lip, revealing long fangs glistening with drool.

"You know we don't feed on children," said Estella. "You're a monster."

"I'm the monster? Oh, that's rich coming from you." Andrew laughed.

While he was momentarily distracted, Estella broke off a chunk of a nearby marble tombstone and flung it at his head. It hit him squarely on the brow and he fell to the ground.

With Andrew out of the way for the time being, Estella turned to the girl. "I'm going to get you out of here, but I have to make sure he won't try and hurt you again. I'm going to put you somewhere safe while I take care of this, OK?"

The girl nodded and Estella picked her up. She ran back to the mausoleum and kicked open the lock. She carried the girl inside and set her down.

"What's your name?" asked Estella.

"Nevaeh," sniffled the girl.

"OK. Listen, Nevaeh. I'm going to shut the door to this place. Don't be scared. There's nothing in here that can hurt you. I'll be back for you in a little bit, so just stay here and don't come out, no matter what."

Nevaeh nodded, and Estella ran back to where she'd left Andrew. He was gone.

She looked around frantically, hoping he hadn't followed her to where she'd left Nevaeh. Then, from the darkness, Andrew lunged at her. Estella managed to sidestep him, and he flew past her. He landed with a roll and sprung to his feet. Estella felt the rage sweep over her again. This time, she embraced it. She felt her teeth sharpen into fangs and her nails lengthen into black claws.

She bolted toward him with a roar. But he was ready for her and slammed her sideways into a large monument. Estella's head swam for a moment, but she quickly recovered. Andrew lunged for her neck, trying to sink his fangs into her throat. Estella caught hold of his head before he could bite her. As he gnashed his fangs at her ravenously, Estella yanked his head to one side, snapping his neck. She kept on twisting until his head popped off with a thick, wet rip.

Estella tossed the head aside and grabbed his limp body. Blood gushed from the neck stump. She stuck her face into the flow and sated her thirst, like a parched woman drinking from a spring. She didn't want any temptations when she returned to Nevaeh, so she drank until she felt like a tick about to pop.

When Andrew's body had served its purpose, she left it lying in the middle of the graveyard. Normally, she didn't like to litter, but his corpse would send a message to her people's foe: *If we would do this to one of our own, we would have no problem doing it to you.*

Estella walked back to the mausoleum where she'd left Nevaeh, trying her best to clean the blood from her face. She didn't want to frighten the girl any more tonight. But when she opened the mausoleum door, Nevaeh was nowhere in sight.

A sharp pain in her chest made Estella gasp. She looked down. The long stick that Nevaeh had been swinging at Andrew now stuck out from between her breasts.

Neveah stepped around in front of her. "Thanks for

taking care of that jerk for me. I was hoping you two would finish each other off actually. Still, one vampire—especially a sentimental one—is much easier to kill than two."

Estella slumped to the floor, gasping.

"It looks like my aim was a bit off," said Nevaeh. "Let me help you with that."

She slowly pulled the stake out of Estella's chest, then jammed it back in an inch or so to the left of the original wound. Estella collapsed, and Nevaeh walked over her, whistling as she went.

A Full Moon On Halloween

The full moon hung in the midnight sky, pallid as a skull. Dead leaves skittered across the concrete, whispering in their secret language. I was too old for trick or treating, but I'd gone out wearing a monster mask to cause trouble.

During my shenanigans, I'd met a beautiful girl who wore no costume. She had joined in my mischief, and now we walked through the neighborhood telling scary stories.

"They say when the moon is full on Halloween night, the Devil walks abroad," she said.

"Who says that?"

"I do," said the Devil, ripping off its beautiful girl mask.

The Yule Cat

Brayden hated spending Christmas in Iceland with his aunt and cousin. The only present he'd gotten this year was a new pair of socks. Brayden had a tantrum and threw the socks outside, ignoring his cousin's warnings about the Yule Cat.

Late that night, he awoke to an ear-splitting yowl. Staring in through the second-story window were a pair of gigantic feline eyes. Brayden screamed.

The next morning, his cousin went to wake up him. The bedroom window was open, the blankets were in shambles, and Brayden was gone. The only things left behind were several long, black cat hairs.

Happy Holidays from Charme Cove!

"You have to choose one of us," the two conventionally attractive men said in unison.

Celia Charme wound a lock of her auburn hair around her index finger as she contemplated her choice. On the right was Travis, her boyfriend from New York. He had dark hair and wore a wool peacoat and an expensive cashmere scarf. On the left was Hunter, her high school sweetheart from here in Charme Cove. He had light hair and wore a denim jacket trimmed with Sherpa. His feet were clad in worn cowboy boots despite the fact that there wasn't a farm for miles around.

Celia hadn't wanted to come home to Charme Cove for the annual Winter Festival, but it was the 250th anniversary of the town's founding, and she was required to be there. She was a descendant of the town's founder, Ezekiel Charme, and it was written in the town bylaws that a Charme must be present at least every fifty years to conduct the festival. She'd been so busy with her job as a writer at a fashion magazine in New York that she'd forgotten all about her obligations back home. Several work deadlines were coming due all at the same time and going back to Charme Cove meant that she might not make those deadlines, but traditions had to be honored or else there would be consequences.

How could she choose between the two men that she loved? They were both good choices, even though they were so different. Travis was a serious businessman but could also be kind and thoughtful. Hunter was a fun-loving free spirit who also happened to make good money selling handcrafted wooden trinkets. Travis had blue eyes. Hunter had green eyes. Travis was clean shaven. Hunter had a beard, but not one that was big enough to look intimidating. The two men stood before her like two hunks of wood that also happened to be hunks in the "attractive" sense of the word. They stared at her.

Soon, a crowd of town folk had formed around the trio, all looking to Celia for her decision. Old women in shawls stared at her, and young couples holding hands stared at her, and one small child with eyes like a soulful seal stared at her. All those eyes on her made Celia nervous, as well as creeped her the fuck out. Finally, she took a deep breath and answered them all.

"I choose...both of you!"

The men looked confused, but the rest of the town cheered. "Appeasement for the Aberration! Appeasement for the Aberration!" they chanted. They swarmed over the men and bound them tightly with ropes. They carried them off through the brightly lit, snow-covered streets of Charme Cove.

Several strong men from among the town folk lifted Celia on their shoulders and followed the rest of the crowd. The procession wound its way through the streets, picking up cheering and chanting people along the way. Travis and Hunter wriggled in their bonds, trying to escape, but never let it be said that the people of Charme Cove don't know how to bind up a man! The men yelled to be released, and their yelling mingled with the roar of the townspeople. Loudest of all was Celia's voice, intoning the ancient Song of the Aberration:

"Gnashoth the Aberration, we summon thee!
From the depths of the sea, from the vast starry void,
Come forth unto us, thou foul, thou unclean!
Sacrifices we offer thee, for appeasement, for favor.
Show yourself unto us, O Aberrant One!
Y'shah! Y'shah! Gnashoth Iliag!"

It was a song that had been taught to her as a small child in preparation for this day, and she sang it well.

The throng made its way to the waterfront, where dozens of boats adorned with twinkling lights waited for them. They threw the sacrifices into two smaller craft, and Celia was set gently down on a throne in the bow of the most ornate among them. Then off they rowed.

After a few minutes, they had reached their destination—a small island in the middle of the cove. The island was too small for most of the town folk to gather on, so they waited in their boats while the bound men were dragged onto shore and laid down upon the stone of sacrifice. Celia stepped gracefully onto the island and walked over to them. They pleaded with her to spare their lives, but she paid them no heed.

Turning to face the vast abyss of the ocean, Celia held her arms out and chanted once again. "Y'shah! Y'shah! Gnashoth Iliag!"

The ocean began to roil. From out of its depths came the cyclopean bulk of Gnashoth the Aberration. In form, Gnashoth most resembled an unshelled snail. Its eyes, of which there were hundreds, rose on stalks from its head. Along its sides were myriad tentacles lined with suckers, each ending in serrated pinchers. Gnashoth undulated its way onto the shore, its every grotesque movement an abomination to all that was good and holy in the world.

Travis and Hunter screamed. The people of Charme Cove cheered. Celia chanted. The Aberration emitted a ululating cacophony and swallowed up both men in one gulp. Then Gnashoth returned to the sea from whence it came, appeased for yet another fifty years.

Celia wiped a tear of gratitude from her eye. It was good to be home for the holidays.

THE RETURN

"It's not human!" cried Daisuke. "Not anymore!"

The apparition floated before Daisuke and Ken. Its long ebony hair obscured its features, and it was clad in a white robe that pooled on the floor.

"It's Megumi..." said Ken, wonderingly. "She's come back for me."

Daisuke backed away as it approached.

Ken embraced the figure, brushing the hair out of its face. A bone-white visage glared back at him with black-rimmed eyes. Megumi shrieked with rage, wrapping her shrouded arms around Ken, who screamed in terror. Then both of them disappeared.

"You really shouldn't have cheated on her, man," said Daisuke.

The Catacombs

Aiden followed Ricky through the labyrinthian basement of the abandoned factory.

"Where are we going?" Aiden asked.

"To the catacombs. It's really cool," said Ricky.

The teens wandered around the derelict building until they reached a dark room. Ricky ushered Aiden inside. The only light was near the entrance, where it trickled in from the hallway. The door slammed shut. Aiden yelled.

"Chill out," said Ricky, switching on a light. It flickered on, revealing rows of metal shelving filled with bloody severed heads.

"I couldn't visit the ones in Paris, so I made my own," Ricky whispered in Aiden's ear.

What Lies Beyond

I lurked in the dim hallway of the seedy apartment building, hesitant to knock on the scratched black door. Even in the murky light, I felt vulnerable and exposed. I pulled out my phone and checked the time: 2:34 a.m. When I'd received Alex's text an hour ago, I'd told myself not to even open it, let alone respond. Then, like a jump cut from a movie, I'd found myself here. My heart thudded anxiously as I debated whether to just go back home without knocking.

In the end, the decision was made for me when the door was yanked open, and Alex stuck their head out into the hallway. I jerked backward with a gasp, not just because of the sudden movement, but also because of Alex's appearance. Granted, I hadn't seen them in over a year, so maybe I'd forgotten how gaunt they were or how dark were the circles under their eyes. But I hadn't forgotten the intensity of those red-rimmed eyes, sea-glass green, glittering with dark humor.

"Sam!" they said. "I was beginning to think you'd changed your number! I thought I was going to have to come collect you myself. But then I thought to myself, 'What if Sam went and moved on me as well as changed her number?' But I know you. You never change. That's what I like about you. I'm always changing, always shifting, like shadows thrown by candlelight. But you're steady. And that's why I need you, Sam. You're my control in this experiment."

My face must have betrayed my feelings, because Alex laughed and continued: "See? Already I can tell just by observing your reactions, how you look at me, how you wrap your arms around yourself, that you're afraid. That's OK, that's fine. You always were a bit afraid of me, weren't you, babe? But that didn't stop you from coming, and that's what's important. I knew I could always count on you to come. But don't keep lurking on my threshold—I've got so much to show you, love. So much."

Alex said this in their usual flash flood of words. Before I had time to catch my breath, they gripped my wrist and pulled me inside the apartment like a kelpie dragging its victim below deep-green waters.

Last time I'd been here, the interior of Alex's apartment had resembled a kelpie's lair too. It had been swathed in shades of deep teal, turquoise, cerulean, and indigo. Candles in ornate mercury-glass containers had shimmered against the pale-blue walls. The shifting sea of colors had pulled at me like a tidal wave, and trying to leave was like trying to swim to the ocean's surface without knowing which direction was up.

I'd managed to reemerge into the world outside their

grotto eventually, gasping and panting as if I really did swim for my life. In a way, I had. Being with Alex was like slowly drowning and loving it. I'd promised myself I'd never be involved with them again, and to their credit, they let me go without contacting me until this night. All these months I'd prided myself on my restraint and self-preservation and it turned out I could only resist Alex until they called me.

As they ushered me into the apartment, I expected to feel submerged again. I flinched as glaring yellow light assaulted my eyes.

"Yeah, I've redecorated a bit since you were here last," Alex said, noticing my surprise. "You like it?"

"It's... bright," I said, which was an understatement. The formerly blue walls were painted a shade of yellow that looked like a number 2 pencil with the saturation dialed to eleven, a color so loud it practically screamed. Alex must have done the paintwork themself because long trails and drips of paint had hardened on the walls, and pools of paint had spilled onto the wooden floors. Alex didn't have the patience to put down drop cloths or wait for each coat of paint to dry.

The furniture was draped in yards of yellow crushed velvet. All the floor pillows, poufs, and candles which had previously filled the living room were gone. Presumably they'd been piled on the couch and covered with fabric, because its form was lumpy and uneven. The only remaining furniture that actually looked usable was a card table and two folding chairs. The table was covered in a yellow satin tablecloth and the two chairs were clad in matching—but ill-fitting—chair covers.

"Of course it's bright!" Alex said from the kitchen, which had also been painted yellow, including all the appliances. The espresso machine growled. "How were we supposed to stay awake with all the blues and greens I had in here?" Alex yelled over the din. "I mean, do you know how low the vibrational frequency of blue is? I mean, it's practically zero!" Alex laughed manically, the sound especially loud and brash after the coffee machine had shut off.

I wondered where they were getting their information about color vibration. I'd had a period where I was into chakras, and what they said didn't match what I'd learned. Most likely, they'd just made it up.

Alex walked back into the living room with two mugs full of coffee. They nodded toward the card table, indicating I should sit down. I did so, and Alex placed a mug in front of me and sat down in the other chair.

"Go ahead, drink up," they urged.

I took a sip and grimaced at the bitterness, just as Alex blurted out "Oh, wait!"

Alex bolted out of their chair and back into the kitchen. They emerged a few seconds later with a bag of sugar. They leapt gracefully back to the table and spooned five heaping teaspoons into my mug, spilling a bunch of sugar onto the tablecloth in their haste. They dumped a similar amount of sugar into their own mug, used the same spoon to stir both our coffees, then tossed it back into the sugar bag.

"OK, now drink up," Alex said breathlessly.

I took a sip. The combination of sugar and caffeine galvanized me, obliterating any remaining vestiges of sleepiness. In the time it took me to take one sip, Alex gulped down their entire mug. They slammed the mug back down on the table and began drumming their long fingers, eyes bright and hectic.

"So! Where was I? Oh yes! Colors and their vibrational frequencies. For our purposes, blue and green are right out. Too slow. We need fast colors. But not just fast colors—the fastest color. And what could be faster than yellow? Yellow is the brightest color the human eye can perceive. It stands to reason then that it must have the highest vibrational frequency of any color. Sam, stay with me. I can see your eyes glazing over. Drink your coffee."

I needed no further encouragement, and continued to drink as Alex spoke.

"I mean, scientists have proven the emotional effects colors have on humans. But what about the physical effects? That's what I started thinking about. It was one of those nights when I couldn't sleep to save my life. It had been piss pouring for days, and my yellow raincoat was draped over the chair in the bedroom. My eyes kept being drawn back to it, even in the darkness, with just the lights from the street. I lay there and I stared at this coat for hours, trying to figure out what was so compelling about it. You know how fast my thoughts fly when I'm concentrating, so I'm not going to tell you all the concepts and ideas I formulated during that time because we'd be here for weeks.

"But in short, I noticed that the yellow of the coat was keeping me awake, alert. What's more, it was awakening and alerting other senses I didn't even know I had. I could see the layers of this reality flaking away like the layers of an onion. I could almost see what lies beyond this reality. I sat there, straining my perception, my heart lurching in excitement and fear. And just as I was about to watch that final layer peel away, my body succumbed to exhaustion and I awoke several hours later to find this mundane world had once again reasserted its stranglehold on my mind."

My heart galloped like a racehorse. Not only because of the immense amount of caffeine I'd now consumed, but also because I'd heard these kinds of stories from Alex before. I knew what they meant.

"Alex..." I began.

Alex continued as if I hadn't spoken. "So I thought to myself, 'I need more yellow!' See, if just that little bit of yellow in my raincoat could trigger such a strong reaction in me, how much more would a whole apartment of yellow affect me? So I took my coat down to the hardware store and I had them color-match it. They had this great sale on their paint—buy one five-gallon bucket, get one half-price—so I bought four buckets. I was gonna buy all my paint supplies there too, but their prices on brushes were ridiculous. It was total bullshit, and I told them that. Have a big sale on paint and then jack up the prices on your brushes? That's bullshit. They didn't like me calling them out, and I almost got into a fight with the manager, but I was like 'Fuck this shit' and I flung a wad of cash at them and stormed out. I ended up buying my brushes at the flea market..."

"Alex, are you still taking your meds?" I asked. I knew damn well what the answer was, but I was too timid to accuse them directly.

Alex's expression darkened, and I tensed up in anticipation of their reaction. My blood pressure rose so much it felt like my head was going to explode. Alex must have noticed my distress because their features quickly smoothed back into the same charming smile that first won me over.

"Sam, you know those pills dull my thinking. I'm like a golem when I'm on them. If I'd been taking those pills, I never would have had this revelation," Alex said. "Now back to what I was saying about the paint..."

I slid my chair out from the table, the metal legs scraping harshly across the hardwood floor. I strode to the door without saying a word, without looking back. My hand was on the doorknob when I felt Alex grab my other wrist, their grip clammy and strong. I didn't turn around.

"You know this is why I left the last time," I said, my voice trembling slightly. "You know I can't be with you when you're like this." I tried to pull my wrist out of their grasp, but their thin fingers clamped down harder.

"Sam, I need your help with this. I didn't get a chance to tell you yet, but what I'm doing, it's dangerous."

"Then don't fucking do it!" I yelled, still not looking at them.

"I have to," Alex said softly. "How can I stop when I

89

could be so close to figuring out the secrets of what lies beyond this reality?"

I gritted my teeth and jerked out of Alex's grip. I'd yanked the door open and had one foot over the threshold already when Alex said, "What happens if you leave and something bad happens to me? What if I do have another breakdown? What if I die? How can you leave knowing you could have stayed and saved me? How are you going to live with that? Look at me."

I turned around. Alex's sea foam eyes were brimming with tears. I had never hated and loved someone so much in my life. I wasn't worried about whatever manic delusion Alex had invented, but they clearly hadn't slept in days. They probably hadn't had anything but coffee for the last few days either. What if Alex hurt themselves during one of their hallucinations? What if they got so paranoid that they thought the only relief was slitting their wrists or OD'ing on their unused meds? I was probably the only one who visited Alex. If they died, who knew how long it would be before they were found? And what sort of state would they be in? Grisly images filled my mind, and my eyes began to burn with tears.

Alex stared intensely at me, and I couldn't resist any longer. I burst out crying, and Alex wrapped me in a tight hug. I laid my head on their shoulder and sobbed, wishing I could will them out of this state.

"Just stay with me for the weekend," they whispered. "Just for the weekend, and if we don't make any progress by

Monday morning, I swear I'll start taking my meds again. Just trust me again for a little while longer."

"OK," I said, letting go of Alex so I could wipe my eyes. I looked at them. Their eyes were placid and free from tears.

"Great," they said, a satisfied smile playing across their lips. "Let's get started."

The next several hours passed in a frenetic blur. The memories form a jaundiced, impressionistic haze in my mind. I know we drank endless cups of strong coffee, the roar of the coffee machine like the bass line of the soundtrack to those hours. We danced to looping electro swing playlists online, and if it bothered any of Alex's neighbors, we took no notice. The boundaries between day and night wore away, leaving only one continuous moment of now.

Once, when the sky was dark and the stars shone feebly, we made a run to a twenty-four-hour convenience store. Literally a run, our shoes slapping the pavement, our breathing ragged and joyous. We needed to bring yellow with us, or risk losing all the progress we'd made. I made a poncho out of the tablecloth and Alex wore the yellow raincoat that instigated this whole ordeal.

The cashier must've thought we were on drugs when we burst through the doors, our exuberant laughter verging on screams. But I want to stress that we were never on any drugs unless you count caffeine and sugar. We bought up all their coffee, all their sugar, and as many energy drinks as we could carry. The trip back should have taken much longer than it did, burdened as we were. We had energy to spare though, and ran back to Alex's apartment, huffing and puffing from our exertion.

I couldn't tell you how long we stayed awake. I know it was until Monday at least because I got a call from my boss. I let the call go to voicemail because at that point, I was completely invested in Alex's experiment. We spent hours excitedly discussing the nature of reality and how thin it was once the mind was properly stimulated. My heart thudded and lurched, and my hands jittered and flapped faster than the up-tempo music that blared in the background of all our conversations. I wasn't sure if death or revelation would come first, or whether they might not be one and the same.

Then all the yellow in the room brightened beyond its normal intensity. The walls dripped and melted like honey, leaving behind a shade of yellow I'd never seen before. It gleamed and glimmered prismatically. It was beautiful and terrible to behold.

"This is it!" Alex cried, their eyes alight with religious fervor. "We're about to break through the bonds of this reality. Sam, are you ready?"

I couldn't form any coherent reply. I just gasped like a fish yanked from its aquatic environs into a world utterly alien to it. A sizzling black line appeared in the air in front of us, delineating a jagged arch. Through the arch drifted in the thumping bass of techno music, accompanied by the strange and haunting melodies of unfamiliar instruments.

Alex gripped my hand tightly in their clammy grasp and pulled me toward the archway. "Come on! This is the culmination of everything we've worked for. You can't back out now. Don't you want to see?"

Staring into that rip in reality felt like standing on the edge of a bridge, preparing to jump off. But I looked into Alex's eyes. I couldn't let them jump alone. I was all in, for better or worse. I nodded, and Alex laughed in excitement. They reached out and grabbed hold of the tear in the fabric of our world and pulled it back like a tent flap. A section of the wall peeled away on the flap, and a wave of dizziness swept over me. Alex ran through the portal, dragging me along with them.

On the other side was pandemonium, a sea of people pressed up against one another. The crowd undulated in time with the music, which blared from every direction. All the revelers were dressed in varying shades of yellow, from saffron to dandelion, from lemon to ocher. The outfits themselves were phantasmagorical creations. Many people wore elaborate hats and headdresses, and those that wore no hats had intricate hairstyles in all the colors of the rainbow.

The whole scene resembled a rave set in Las Vegas. The same prismatic yellow that had emanated from the portal gleamed from millions of lights around us. Gold metallic draperies hung on the walls, which stretched up at least a hundred feet to a ceiling coated with shimmering gold. Chandeliers with impossible geometry dangled from the ceiling. Trying to trace the lines of the fixtures made my head pound with confusion.

All this information poured into my consciousness

within a few seconds. My system was overloaded as I tried to make sense of this new world, but Alex pushed through the crowd and began dancing wildly.

"Come on, dance with me!" they yelled over the din. I didn't want to lose them in this mob of strange people, so I sidled my way across the floor until I reached them. They pulled me close, grinding up against me to the beat of the eerie music. Lust growled through me and I pulled Alex into a passionate kiss. Everything else faded away—the glaring lights, the thumping music, the smell of exotic perfume mingled with sweat—nothing mattered in this moment but the taste of Alex's lips on mine, the feel of their body pressed up against me.

We danced for hours and never grew weary. If anything, we had more energy now than before we entered this strange place. We might have danced for hours more if we hadn't been stopped by two beautiful women clad in golden dresses.

"Pardon us for interrupting your fun, but I don't believe we've met," said one woman, who had long red hair woven in a multitude of braids. She wore a harlequin mask and a smile a person would die for. "I'm Camilla," she said, with a curtsy.

I curtsied back, lifting the hem of my tablecloth poncho. Alex bowed with a flourish.

"And I'm Cassilda," said the second woman. Her raven hair was styled like a ziggurat, and a yellow damask half-mask covered the left side of her face. She nodded curtly at us, and we did likewise. Despite the raging music and the roar of the crowd, the women spoke in a normal tone of voice, and we still heard them perfectly.

"I'm Alex, and this is Sam," Alex said. "It's a pleasure to meet you both. This place is absolutely crazy. I've never been any place like this before, except maybe in my dreams, and I know I'm not dreaming because Sam and I have been awake for... for I don't know how long, but it's been a long time. We've been experimenting, trying to pull back the layers of our reality, and I guess it worked because here we are. By the way, where exactly are we?"

Camilla smiled. "You're in the court of the King in Yellow," she said.

"Who's the King in Yellow?" I asked.

"I am," said a jovial voice from behind us. Alex and I jumped and spun around. Standing in front of us was a man—at least they seemed to be a man—draped in a saffron velvet hooded robe. The folds of the robe spread across the floor like a train and the sleeves covered his hands. He wore a golden crown perched jauntily over the hood of his robe, and an alabaster mask covered his face. The mask was fixed in a too-wide, sardonic smile, and had eye slits like upturned crescent moons and black eyebrows that seemed to be arched sarcastically. The holes in the mask were large enough that I should have been able to see some of his features through them, but all I could see was a deep black void.

Camilla and Cassilda both curtsied, and Alex and I followed their lead, making similar gestures of deference.

The King acknowledged our greetings with a regal nod of his head. Then he threw an arm around Alex and me and lead us through the crowd, which parted in front of him.

"Yes, welcome to my court here in lovely Carcosa," said the King.

"Carcosa? Where's that? Is this some sort of alternate dimension?" asked Alex.

"Alternate? No, Carcosa is located at the nexus of all dimensions, all universes," said the King.

"Wow," I said. Always the stunning conversationalist. But I was too overwhelmed by the blazing lights, the thumping music, and the roar of the crowd to contribute anything of value.

"Wow indeed, Sam," said the King. "So what brings the two of you to my court?"

Alex went into enthusiastic detail about our experiment, about their theories on color vibrations, and anything else that crossed their mind. Most people would be looking for a polite way to escape the conversation when Alex rambled manically like this. Even I was getting a bit tired of listening to them. But Camilla and Cassilda and even the King seemed enthralled by Alex's pontificating.

"Fascinating!" said the King when Alex had finally stopped talking. "You are a true experimentalist, Alex. Most of my courtiers are artists, writers, musicians, degenerate hedonists... but a person of science is a rare find. And you, Sam. A loyal friend is an even rarer find, even among the more mundane dimensions. I hope you enjoy your time in my court, and that you would consider becoming my newest courtiers."

I knew I should feel flattered by the King's praise. Alex was bouncing on the balls of their feet, but I couldn't shake a feeling of discomfort. It was like being complimented by a creepy uncle—I could tell an ulterior motive lurked behind it. Maybe if the King hadn't been wearing such a disturbing mask, I would've felt better about him, but something inside me was still wary. Still, it wouldn't do to be impolite...

"Thank you," I replied, trying my best to smile genuinely. Then my stomach rumbled loudly enough that it could be heard even over the crowd and the music. I flushed with embarrassment.

"How rude of me not to offer our newest guests food and drink!" said the King. "Camilla, Cassilda, do you think the rest of the courtiers could do with refreshments as well?"

"Yes, my liege," said Camilla. "We've been dancing for... how long has it been?" she asked, turning to Cassilda.

Cassilda looked off into the distance as if calculating. "Oh, it's been at least a century, I suppose. It's so hard to tell in Carcosa"

"Then I'd say it's time for a bit of a break," said the King. He clapped his robe-shrouded hands. Even though the sound was muffled, it rang throughout the hall. The music stopped and the crowd's roar muted to a mumble.

"Time to dine, my courtiers fine!" the King said.

The crowd parted, lining up along the walls. Camilla and Cassilda escorted us to one side, while the King walked to the front of the room and sat on an ornate golden throne. He clapped his hands again and dozens of long tables covered in yellow tablecloths like the one I was wearing appeared in the center of the room. The tables were laden with golden dishes full of food and goblets full of wine.

"Help yourself!" cried the King. "Feast to your heart's content!"

"Come on, friends!" said Cassilda, grabbing hold of Alex and myself. "We want to make sure we get a good seat."

We joined the crowd running toward the tables. Cassilda and Camilla ran ahead of us, shouldering the other courtiers out of the way, even knocking several people to the floor in their haste. It was a mad scramble to get a seat at the tables, but everyone was laughing as they shoved and pushed each other. Even the people trampled on the floor were laughing. I found myself giggling breathlessly too as Alex and I searched for a place to sit.

"Over here!" called Camilla. Across the table from her and Cassilda were two open seats. Another couple of courtiers saw them at the same time as Alex and me. We eyed each other from across the room and then I shot a look to Alex from the corner of my eye. They caught my look and grinned. Alex let out a bloodcurdling yell and began charging toward the seats. I ran after them, bellowing like a dinosaur. The courtiers were caught off guard at first, but quickly recovered and ran at us. From several feet away, Alex flung themself across both chairs.

"No fair! You can't take more than one seat!" said one of the courtiers.

Alex slid their legs off one of the chairs and I plopped down immediately. They pushed themself up in the remaining chair until they were straddling it backward and waggled their fingers in a sarcastic wave at the defeated courtiers. I stuck out my tongue. They slunk off to find other seats at another table.

Cassilda and Camilla clapped. Alex turned around until they were facing forward in their chair. They mimed buffing their nails on their shirt sleeve.

"That was brilliant, you two," said Camilla. "I'm so glad you managed to beat Harold and Victoria to those seats. They're such bores. I surely would have killed myself if I'd had to listen to their inane blathering all night," she said.

"Please don't kill yourself," said Cassilda, piling her plate full of rolls from a basket in front of her. "It'd be much better to kill them."

"True," replied Camilla. "It would be best for everyone if I killed them. They're beginning to wear out their welcome. Soon the King will probably sic the Hounds on them. I'd be doing them a kindness, really."

I laughed, but Cassilda said "Oh, don't bring up the Hounds at dinner, my dear. Thinking on them for too long puts me off my food."

I could see Alex was getting ready to ask more about the subject, but I didn't want to offend our new friends, so I said "Look, Alex! They have sushi! Toss me some, please."

Alex grabbed a sushi roll and lobbed it at me. I managed to catch it in my mouth and ate it.

"I didn't mean it literally," I said, as the people around me applauded my feat.

The feast went on for hours, the food and drink never ending. We had deep conversations with Cassilda and Camilla about Carcosa, the lake of Hali, and the Yellow Sign. They even hinted at the true nature of the King in Yellow, but refused to say anything further when Alex pressed them for more information. Camilla cleared her throat loudly and inclined her head toward the King's throne.

I turned my head slightly and saw the King in Yellow staring our way, his arm propped up on the throne and his head resting on his hand. A chill ran down my spine. That fixed smile on his mask unnerved me.

Then from some unseen portion of the ballroom there sounded the gonging of an enormous clock. Its peals were deep and ominous. All conversation stopped as the clock tolled on, like a portent of doom. When the clock tolled twelve, the King in Yellow rose from his throne and clapped his hands.

"The time has come. Unmask!" he bellowed.

The assembled guests removed their masks.

Cassilda and Camilla were so beautiful, they made my heart throb with desire. I looked around the rest of the room. Some of the uncovered faces were almost as lovely as theirs, but others were grotesque, inhuman monstrosities. Alex could sense my distress because they grabbed my face and directed it to theirs.

"Don't look at them. Just look at me," they whispered. I

did so, staring intently into their oceanic eyes. My breathing slowed and my nerves calmed. All this strangeness had been exhilarating at first, but I was beginning to long for some normalcy.

"Alex, how do we get home?" I asked.

They paused a moment, thinking.

They were just about to respond when the King spoke again. "You there! Why have you not unmasked?"

I thought for a moment he was referring to Alex and me, but his outstretched arm pointed at a man a few feet from us.

"I'm not wearing a mask, my liege," the man stammered.

"Stand up!" commanded the King. The man stood.

The King strode toward him, his robes whipping behind as if stirred by a breeze, but there was no breeze in the ballroom. The man trembled as the regent approached. Although the King's mask still bore the same exuberant grin, it seemed to exude a clear air of menace now.

"We all wear masks," said the King.

He raised his hands to the man's face. The sleeves of his robes slipped down to his elbows, revealing razor sharp talons. He dug his claws into the man's face, severing skin from muscle. With a yank and a sound like ripping fabric, the King tore off the man's face and flung it behind him. The man let out a shriek that ended in hysterical laughter and then slumped to the floor.

The King surveyed the rest of his courtiers. "Well, what are you waiting for? UNMASK!" he roared.

Camilla took a metal nail file from her purse and jammed it into her cheek. She sawed away at the flesh, blood flowing in rivulets down her neck and onto her breast. Cassilda had a fork and was jabbing it along her forehead. Others had picked up knives or had smashed glasses on the table, using the jagged shards to hack away at their faces.

"Camilla, dear, can you help me out?" asked Cassilda, still stabbing herself with the fork.

"Of course! Just give me a moment." Camilla finished sawing with her file, then rolled her skin downward like a woman taking off a stocking. She laid the skin on the table and smoothed it out before turning to Cassilda. "A fork? Really?" she asked, rolling her eyes.

Her entire eyeballs rolled as she did this. The muscles in her jaw flexed as she talked, and her exposed teeth moved up and down.

"It was all that was handy!" protested Cassilda. "Look at it this way: I perforated it to make things easier for you."

Camilla tsked and stuck the file into Cassilda's forehead, cutting along the line dotted in blood. My stomach writhed like a basket full of eels as I watched, but I couldn't seem to look away. Then Alex slipped their hand in mine and squeezed it. I turned and looked at them to see their green eyes wide with terror. I'd never seen Alex afraid before. It made me want to panic, but I could sense that drawing that kind of attention to us would be a mistake, so I just kept hold of Alex's hand.

Camilla turned to us, her face muscles wet and glistening. "Here, dears. Let me help you. Come closer." She leaned over the table.

I stood up and backed away from her horrific, dripping visage, pulling Alex with me. "Um... thank you, but we actually have to be leaving now. I've got work in the morning," I said lamely.

"Why worry about work when you can stay with us and indulge your every desire?" said Cassilda, grinning toothily at me.

Every fiber of my body screamed at me to run, but my brain knew it was a bad idea. Alex and I kept backing away, mumbling apologies. We took another step backward and bumped into someone. A chill shot down my spine. There was only one person it could be.

We turned around and faced the King in Yellow. The eyeholes of his mask bored into us. I could feel his breath on my face, hot and rancid. His gore-encrusted talons were spread open in a gesture of welcome.

"Alex! Sam! You're still wearing your masks, I see. The party can't continue until all my guests have unmasked. Here, let me help you as I helped our friend Phillipe." The King reached out his talons.

We edged away from him as best we could.

"No, thank you. We're actually... allergic to having our faces removed," said Alex.

"Now, why do I get the feeling you're not being truthful with me?" said the King, cocking his head to the side.

"No, for real!" said Alex, still backing away. "I break out

in hives. Right, Sam?"

"Yeah," I agreed quickly. "Big ol' hives all over. Yeah, the last time I took my face off, it had this godawful rash on it when I put it back on. So we tend to keep our faces, um, on our faces." I giggled helplessly.

The King tilted his head even farther, so that his mask was almost horizontal. I heard the tendons in his neck crack as he moved.

"I'm sorry to hear that, Sam. But if you want to be courtiers of mine, you must unmask. And I feel I must warn you that if you reject my offer, I'll have to release the Hounds," he said apologetically.

I felt Alex stiffen beside me. Their eyes were full of a defiant light. Alex had been off their meds for who knows how long, and I knew they didn't respond well to threats in that state. I put my hand on Alex's shoulder to keep them from doing anything stupid. Alex shrugged out of my grip and strode toward the King.

"If it's so great for everyone to take off their masks, why don't you take off yours, huh? Come on, unmask!" yelled Alex. They grabbed the King's mask and tugged it away.

I wish they hadn't.

Alex had gone completely silent. The rest of the assembled courtier's gasped in horror at Alex's audacity. I winced at Alex's actions, but I felt compelled to look at whatever they had uncovered. So I looked upon the visage of the King in Yellow.

What can I say? What I saw was to some degree de-

scribable, but how do I truly express the soul-freezing horror of it all? What I saw behind the King's mask was like a hole cut in the fabric of the universe, revealing another vast universe inside him. Entire galaxies spiraled madly through that hole. The roiling blackness was full of things—things that looked like deep sea creatures, things that looked like one-celled organisms, and things that could only be described as "things".

I felt myself leaning forward, drawn in like a gravitational pull. I wanted to pull back, but I was compelled onward, leaning further and further. What would happen if I tripped? Would I fall into the abyss that hid inside the King in Yellow? If so, I would likely fall forever, unless I was devoured by one of the many creatures that prowled in the darkness.

The King snatched his mask back from Alex's hand and placed it gently over the cosmic gulf beneath his hood. He chuckled.

"Oh, my dear Sam and Alex! What friends we could have been. But you know the old saying: 'You don't pull the mask off the King in Yellow or your life will surely end.'" He let out a high, multi-tonal whistle.

A deep baying rumbled in the distance and was soon followed by the clicking of claws across the marble floors of the now silent hall. Courtiers made a mass exodus from the room, running, leaping over tables, some tripping and falling, many of them leaving their faces behind like used napkins.

Soon, the ballroom was empty except for Alex, the

King, and me. Oh, and some horrible nightmare creatures that looked like hybrids between emaciated dogs and dragons. Their scaly black skin clung to their skeletons, with little muscle or flesh to pad it out. Their mouths lolled, splitting their faces open from one side to the other. Jagged fangs glistened with drool and baleful red eyes glared at us.

At least a dozen or more of these beasts sidled up to the King, awaiting instruction.

"My Hounds," he said. "The Hounds of Tindalos, to be precise. No matter where you run in this or any other universe, they will find you. Now since I'm a sporting sort, I'll give you a thirty-second head start. Not that it really matters—The Hounds never lose their prey. But it's more fun when the prey thinks it has a chance to escape, don't you agree?"

Alex and I stared at him in silence.

"No, I don't suppose you would," he replied. "But enough chit-chatting! Time to run!" He started counting down from thirty. The Hounds crouched beside him, ready to lunge at his command.

Alex just stood there, tears streaming down their face. "I'm sorry I dragged you into this. I'm so sorry!" they cried.

"It's OK. But we've got to go!" I said, pulling Alex behind me as I started to run. After a moment's hesitation, Alex began running too. I let go of their hand so I could pump both my arms.

Our footsteps thudded across the hall. It was gigantic and brightly lit, with no place to hide.

"We have to get outside! Look for a door, a window, anything," I panted.

The King had reached twenty in his countdown. We didn't have much time left.

"There!" shouted Alex, pointing off to our right. A golden door stood partway open. Glittering blackness gleamed beyond it. I couldn't tell, nor did I care, what we were running into. It couldn't be worse than what we were running away from. We bolted for the door as the King reach ten.

We burst through it and found ourselves outside. A great dark lake shimmered before us. The sky was a deep midnight blue, and the stars twinkled like black diamonds against it. I glanced around to see if there were any boats that would get us across the water, but to no avail. The only things on this shore were the crumbling ruins of once majestic buildings that surrounded us.

Just off to our left, a door to one of the buildings hung open. We bolted inside and slammed the door behind us. A large cabinet stood nearby, so Alex and I grabbed it and scooted it in front of the door. No sooner had we done this than the booming voice of the King, seemingly emanating from everywhere around us, bellowed "ZERO! HOUNDS, DO YOUR WORST!". More faintly, we could hear the snarling and barking of the Hounds as they charged after us.

We hadn't made it far from the ballroom. We moved quietly away from the door, deeper into the abandoned building. It looked like it had once been an opulent mansion, but now the ornate wallpaper hung in tatters from moldy walls. The thick carpet of dust on the hardwood floors helped muffle our steps. We walked down a long hallway filled with portraits of strange people in even stranger clothes. Various rooms branched off on either side, but we kept going straight forward.

"Where are we going?" asked Alex. They hadn't been their usual take-charge self since they'd seen the Hounds. Something in them had broken at that horrible sight, and now they were almost childlike in their dependence on me—which was bad because I'm the last person you want in charge in an emergency. I'm normally prone to panicking and hyperventilating, but seeing Alex in this state triggered my protective side. So I pushed down all my natural instincts that yelled at me to freak out, and I tried to come up with a plan.

"We don't want to get trapped in this building, so we should for a way out. A back door or something," I said.

Just then, the front door began to rattle violently. Hoarse barking came from the other side.

The Hounds had found us.

We ran down the hallway and ended up in a dilapidated kitchen. On the far side of the room, a door stood slightly ajar. Alex ran past me and grabbed hold of it. But before they could open the door, I heard a low snarl.

"NO!" I ran to the door and slammed up against it to try to push it shut. But a Hound had pushed its snout through the opening. It gnashed its teeth at us, slavering with drool. The two of us shoved against the door again, but we were slowly being scooted backward by the Hound. I glanced around desperately and spotted a ratty broom within reach. I grabbed it and began whacking the Hound in the face. It growled and bit down on the broom, nearly yanking it from my hand. I managed to hold on, and we played tug-of-war with the broom for a moment.

I let out a laugh despite myself and I had to bite my tongue to keep from saying "Who's a good boy?"

Eventually, the broom snapped in half and the Hound staggered back. Alex and I took advantage of this to push the door shut. I flipped the lock just as the Hound flung itself against the door, and though it shuddered in its frame, it held. The same could not be said for the front door at the other end of the long hallway, which splintered open under the assault of the other Hounds. They had managed to knock over the cabinet we'd pushed in front of it, and they began pouring in.

I spun around, searching frantically for any alternative exits. A flight of stairs in the corner of kitchen caught my eye.

"That way!" I cried. Alex and I charged up the stairs. They were cluttered with debris that impeded our progress, but I hoped it would at least slow down the Hounds as well. The staircase went up for several flights. We ran past floor after floor, hoping to reach the top. The Hounds clambered after us, panting and growling.

The stairs ended with another long hallway lined with

closed doors. Alex and I pushed and pulled on each of them as we rushed forward but found them all locked. At the very end of the hallway, a ladder hung from a trap door in the ceiling.

Behind us, the Hounds burst out of the staircase, their claws leaving long gouges in the hardwood floor as they galloped down the hall. With no other options, we climbed the ladder.

Alex went first, scrambling up to the room above in a few seconds. I went to follow them, but the ladder was rickety and began to buckle under my weight. I had to climb much more slowly and carefully to make sure the ladder didn't break. I was standing on the last rung, halfway into the attic room, when one of the Hounds lunged up and latched onto the edge of my poncho. It yanked me backward. I lost my grip and fell several feet before I managed to grab hold of one of the rungs again. I managed to swing my legs around so I was standing on the ladder again, but the Hound still had my poncho in its snarling mouth, and the other Hounds were gathering to pounce on me. Whipping off the poncho, I continued to climb as fast as I could.

Above me, Alex held out their hand to help me up and I grabbed it just as the ladder gave way beneath me. The stress of supporting me almost dragged Alex from the attic, but they managed to brace themself while I pulled myself up, my stomach dragging painfully on the lip of the attic opening.

Alex and I sat on the floor, sweating, panting, and

covered in dust. Below us, the Hounds leapt and gnashed their teeth, trying to gain access to the attic. Some of them got disturbingly close. We scooted further away from the opening.

"I don't think they can get up here," said Alex.

"Yeah, but I don't want to stick around and find out. We need to find a way out of here."

"I can't run anymore, Sam. At least not right now. I'm exhausted." Alex's voice was trembling. Tears filled their eyes. "I'm so sorry. I should have never asked you to do this with me. I just wanted to see you again. I missed you so much. You kept me sane, or at least as sane as I can be. I understand why you left though. I'm too much work and I'm not worth it." Alex broke down crying.

"You are worth it," I said. "I should've never left you. Look, we're not good for each other. We're like fire and gasoline—we feed each other's faults. But right now, we're all we've got. I can't have you breaking down on me. I need your crazy intellect to figure out how we can escape from here." I hugged Alex's thin frame.

We embraced for several minutes. It felt good to just relax after days without sleep. The Hounds still leapt and snarled, but the sound was distant and unimportant. Alex pulled away from me, looking around intently.

"Did you see that?" they asked.

"What?"

"That flickering. It almost looked like... That's it!" Alex exclaimed.

"What?!"

"For a moment, I caught a glimpse of my apartment," they said. "I couldn't figure out what happened, but then it hit me. I fell asleep, but only for a moment. It makes perfect sense! If we got here by staying awake, we can go home by falling asleep."

Just then, a Hound leapt high enough to hook its front legs onto the attic floor. It scrabbled, trying to pull itself up.

"I don't think we should fall asleep here," I said as we jumped to our feet.

"There's a window over there!" Alex pointed to one end of the attic.

We ran to the window. It was swollen shut from dampness and wouldn't budge. The Hound had almost wormed its way into the attic. I grabbed a brick from a pile of debris nearby and chucked it through the glass.

Another Hound had joined the first now, writhing its way upward.

Alex and I used another brick to clear the window frame of glass shards. Outside was a small balcony. We climbed out onto it. Several feet away was another house with a balcony attached to it and a pair of French doors leading inside, and even better, they were open. It would be a little tricky, but we should be able to jump over to the other balcony.

Behind us, the Hounds were baying as a couple of them succeeded in pulling themselves through the opening. Alex vaulted smoothly over the balcony railing and onto a small ledge around it. They began walking nimbly toward the other house. I was less graceful. I sat on the edge of the rail, meaning to pivot to the other side, but I lost my balance and flipped over backward. By sheer luck, I caught my feet on the ledge but I flailed my arms, trying to regain my balance. For a moment, I thought I was going to topple over the edge, but Alex grabbed me and steadied me. I smiled at them, and they smiled back wearily.

Then the Hounds poured out onto the balcony, snapping and lunging at us under the rail. Alex pulled me out of the path of their attack and pushed me toward the other house. I scooted as quickly as I could along the ledge, Alex following close behind me. We made it to the point where we would have to jump to reach the next balcony.

"You go first!" said Alex. "You've got longer legs than me—you should be able to jump farther."

I wanted to argue, but the Hounds were already threading their way across the ledge toward us. With no room to back up for a running start, I would probably fall to my death, but facing the Hounds' fury would be worse. I lunged across the gap and slammed into the railing around the other balcony. My hands gripped the rail and I managed to pull myself to my feet, climbing over it and then holding my arms out to Alex, ready to catch them.

Alex leapt like a gazelle. But a Hound reached them mid-leap, sinking its teeth into their side. I leaned over the balcony as far as I could to help them. Their fingertips merely grazed my palm before they and the Hound plunged down to the dark street below.

I screamed in anguish, my heart plummeting along

with Alex. They may have been bad for me, they may have dragged me to this nightmare realm, but I still loved them.

I had little time to mourn, however. Another Hound was preparing to leap across the gap to reach me.

I turned and ran through the open French doors and turned to lock them just as the Hound landed on the balcony. It jumped up, its claws clacking against the glass, but the doors held.

I ran through the house. It was just as dilapidated and abandoned as the previous one. The only difference was that instead of a ladder leading down from the attic, there was a flight of stairs. I hurtled headlong down them, nearly falling a couple of times. I could hear several Hounds on the balcony now, trying to break down the doors.

I needed to find someplace to sleep, even just for a few minutes. Alex had said sleeping was the only way to return home. I couldn't leave this building because I didn't know how many other Hounds were still out there. At least inside, I should be able to barricade myself in somewhere.

At the bottom of the stairs, there was an open door off to my right. I ran inside, hoping I wasn't condemning myself. Once the door was shut, I looked around for something to push in front of it. The room turned out to be a bedroom with a large wardrobe next to the door. It looked sturdier than the cabinet we'd used on the front door, so it might keep out the Hounds long enough for me to fall asleep, even briefly.

I tried to pull it across in front of the door, but it was

too heavy. I went around on the other side of the wardrobe and charged into it with my shoulder. The wardrobe rocked on uneven legs, and I used the momentum to shove it over. It toppled with a crash in front of the door. The Hounds would certainly have heard it fall, but that couldn't be helped.

I scanned the room again. There was a gigantic mahogany four-poster bed against the far wall. Dust lay like another blanket on the ornate yellow bedspread, but I stripped it all off and lay down. The bed creaked beneath me, but it held, and the mattress was surprisingly comfortable. My entire body seemed to sigh with relief as I closed my eyes and curled up against the pillow.

The sound of breaking glass made my eyes pop open and my heart pound. The Hounds must have charged through the attic door and were now thundering down the stairs. With no place to run, I lay as still as possible, trying not to breathe loudly. Maybe the Hounds wouldn't know where I was if I could keep quiet.

The Hounds sniffed and scratched along the floor outside. I held my breath. Dust from the bedsheets tickled my nose and my nostrils burned and itched. Eyes watering, I tried desperately not to sneeze.

Finally, I heard the Hounds gallop down to the floor below. I hid my face in the crook of my arm and sneezed as quietly as I could. I waited for the Hounds to come running back upstairs, but they seemed to continue down through the house.

I closed my eyes again, now desperate for sleep. My mind kept replaying memories from the last few hours, especially the look of despairing surprise on Alex's face as they fell from the roof. Guilt racked my heart. I should have let Alex jump across the gap first. I should have tried harder to catch them, even if it meant falling myself. I never should have agreed to this experiment in the first place. If I hadn't been there to encourage them, Alex would've surely just fallen asleep before anything like this happened.

Even though I was emotionally and physically exhausted, the thoughts racing through my mind meant I couldn't fall asleep. And then I heard an echo of Alex's voice saying, "Breathe with me".

"Breathe with me" used to be our nighttime ritual. I'd started it to help Alex calm themself enough to sleep. We'd breathe together—in for five counts, hold for five counts, out for five counts. After a few minutes of this, we'd always end up falling asleep. I imagined Alex next to me in the bed now. I imagined staring into their green eyes as I'd done so many times before, and I tried not to think about how I'd never gaze into them again. I began to breathe slowly and deeply. In for five, hold for five, out for five. My eyes closed.

I opened my eyes seemingly an instant later. The yellow walls of Alex's apartment blared around me. I had no idea what time or even what day it was. I was lying on the floor, and next to me was Alex. My heart leaped. We'd somehow made it back.

Alex's eyes were closed. They could have been asleep.

I crawled over to them, checking for a pulse, a breath, any sign of life. Then I saw the red pool forming around them. I turned them over and saw a gaping wound rimmed with deep teeth marks on their side.

Tears streamed down my face as I tried to decide what to do. I didn't want to leave Alex alone, but I didn't want to stay in the apartment any longer either. The jaundiced walls overwhelmed me.

I sat there, lost in thought and grief, until I felt reality shift around me. I was suddenly back in the dusty bedroom in Carcosa. The Hounds were tearing through the house looking for me. I blinked hard. I was back in Alex's apartment. What was going on?

The only thing I could think to do was to get more sleep. With that, I should have been able to shake the Hounds.

But I couldn't just leave Alex laying on the cold floor. I took the yellow fabric off the couch, revealing its teal velvet upholstery. After moving all the junk stacked up on it to the floor, I found a powder-blue throw underneath everything. I picked Alex up. They seemed to weigh even less now than they did when they were alive. I laid them down gently on the couch and tucked the blue blanket around them. I kissed their forehead, then turned and left the apartment. I would call the police or an ambulance later, but right now I needed to get to sleep.

I ran from the apartment into the night. No one was around to see me, which was good because I was covered in Alex's blood. My car was still parked by the curb outside.

Fumbling through my pockets, I found my keys then got in the car and drove home. While I was driving, I thought I could hear the Hounds howling in the distance, but I knew they were stuck in that other reality. I told myself it was just regular dogs.

Then a deep bark from behind me made me jump. I looked in the rearview mirror. The reflection showed the Carcosa house. Turning around in my seat, I found myself back on the bed in that hateful room. A Hound was sniffing around outside the barricaded door. Inadvertently, I shifted my weight and the bed creaked beneath me. I froze, but it was too late.

The Hound began clawing at the door. It howled and soon, the other Hounds had joined it, all of them scratching frantically to get to me. I tried blinking again, but it wasn't working.

A sudden jolt brought me back to my world. My seat belt dug into my chest, and the hood of my car was now wrapped around a utility pole. The car had died during the impact, so I turned the keys, trying to get it to start again. The engine wouldn't even act like it was going to turn over. All it did was click at me. Fuck.

The baying of the Hounds warbled behind me, getting clearer and louder every second. I couldn't afford to sit here any longer. I jumped out of the car and ran toward home. Reality flickered in and out around me. Sometimes I was running down a dark street. Then I was back in the bedroom with the Hounds gouging at the wooden door. I stumbled, tripped, even ran face first into the wall of the Carcosa bed-room in my desperation and confusion. Every time I found myself back in Carcosa, I'd close my eyes and breathe until my reality snapped back into place around me.

Finally, I made it home. The universe still shifted wildly, and I flipped back and forth between dimensions so fast it made my head spin. I stumbled to my bedroom and locked the door behind me, pushing a dresser in front of it. Crawl-ing into bed, I pulled the covers over my head and tried to breathe calmly. If I could just fall asleep…

Even with my eyes closed, I could feel the world flicker-ing around me like a silent movie. The Hounds were breaking through the bedroom door. There were no Hounds. A yel-low light, bright and sickly, burned my eyes even through my closed lids. Then blackness again. The worlds spun around me until all the worlds were one: Carcosa.

Still, I kept my eyes shut against that baleful light. Footsteps approached as the light grew brighter. Somehow I knew what it heralded; The King in Yellow drew nigh. I shrank down under the covers, as if they would save me.

"Sam!" called the King. "Didn't I tell you my Hounds would find you no matter where you fled? I am sorry about the loss of your friend, Alex. They would have made an ex-cellent courtier. As would you. But alas, it's too late for that now."

The Hounds chewed their way through the door. It was pointless to run. I put my hands over my eyes and pressed down, shutting out the yellow blaze. Swirling blues, teals, and greens whirled before my vision until they resolved themselves into the exact green of Alex's eyes. I smiled, despite everything.

"Breathe with me," I whispered.

Breathe in, hold, breathe out.

Breathe in, hold, breathe out.

Breathe in...

<u>THE END</u>

About The Author

Sarah Matthews writes horror, dark fantasy, comedy, anything that strikes her fancy, really. She has been published in anthologies by Eerie River Publishing and Black Hare Press. Sarah lives in southern Indiana with her two cats, Luna and Dory.

Follow her on Twitter @superbfinch.